I WISH I WERE SPECIAL

Southern Scandal #1

Julia McBryant

The characters and events portrayed in this book are fictitious. Any similarity to real persons, living or dead, is coincidental and not intended by the author.

ISBN-13: 9781672837927
ISBN-10: 1477123456

Library of Congress Control Number: 2018675309
Printed in the United States of America

for Joey, who pulled me out of the pool

CONTENTS

CHAPTER 1

Quinn Rutledge has plans tonight.

He pulls on his favorite tight white T-shirt and leather pants, clothes that show off his ass, his coltish long limbs and his lean muscle earned from long hours in the saddle. He flat-irons his shoulder-length, Barbie-blond hair pin-straight, ready to swirl and pick up the black light in the club, then meticulously lines his big blue eyes in black. He smudges the liner to perfection. Quinn will definitely end out the night getting fucked. Too bad he couldn't convince Henry Culliver to come with him, but Henry's all wrapped up with Gray Hendricks. Wills *and* Crispin are both staying in Athens for the goddamn summer. So Quinn goes to Club Metro alone. Won't be the first time, won't be the last.

He takes a car from his posh apartment on Bull and East Liberty, all modern lines and sleek steel beams. Quinn has a plan: get trashed, get a guy, get fucked, and kick his ass out. He keeps condoms and lube downstairs and up, plus a fully stocked bar. Quinn knows how to entertain. Quinn also knows how to party, and those leather pants have some coke and ecstasy tucked in a front pocket: he doesn't want to ruin the lines of his ass. He won't be taking any; he's getting up early to foxhunt in the morning. But he'll happily share.

Quinn slides in the door. His fake says South Carolina. Everyone's fake says South Carolina. You'd think the bouncers would have caught on by now, but plausible deniability makes the world go round. The bass pounds in his chest, echoes in his ears and seems to change some vital bodily rhythms. Quinn tosses his card at the bartender, orders a scotch and soda, then sits backwards on one of the ancient barstools and spins slightly back and forth. Eye-linered twinks dance in cages; leather daddies cruise the floor; couples gyrate on each other. Normal guys hang out and take in the scene. Sketchy-looking dudes hang out in corners. Altogether a regular night at Club Metro. A tall, muscular guy in a ripped shirt and jeans sidles up and takes the seat next to him. "Buy you a drink?" he asks.

"Sure," Quinn says. This one looks good: easy-peasy tonight. Dark hair, dark eyes, pretty mouth. Quinn flicks his eyes down. Under tight jeans, he can see the outline of a cock.

"Name's Justin," Ripped Shirt says. "Whatcha drinking?"

Justin: simple. Quinn won't forget that one. "Quinn," he says. "Just started a scotch and soda, so I'll take a shot if you want."

"Shot sounds good," Justin says. "Pick your poison, son."

Son. Justin looks about six years older than Quinn's nineteen. "Tequila," Quinn says wickedly, because he can hold it fine and it drives most people crazy. He reflects that he ought not to take a crazy guy home with him, then pushes the thought out of his mind.

Justin gulps and orders them both a shot of tequila: the cheaper stuff — ugh. Quinn spins on the cracked Naugahyde stool. "So what d'you do, Justin?" he asks.

When Justin shrugs, his biceps ripple deliciously. Probably a gym rat but Quinn's had his share of those. "Insurance. What about you?"

"Savannah School of Art. Equestrian studies."

"Hence the nice ass," Justin says.

"How can you tell if I have a nice ass? I'm sitting on it," Quinn shoots back.

"I watched you walk in the door. Bet you look good in those breeches."

"Baby, you've got no fucking idea." The tequila arrives. Quinn counts it and they throw it down. He beats Justin. Usual. He beats everyone but Henry and Wills Culliver. The twins can take anyone when it comes to shots.

"Love to see you in those breeches," Justin says. He stares at Quinn in the low light. "Love to take them off you even more."

"Would you?" Quinn asks. He lowers his chin and looks up. They all like that, and they all fall for it. Easiest trick in the book.

"You promise to get hard in them for me?"

"We might could arrange that." Of course he'll get rock-hard in those breeches — he's an exhibitionist at heart. He throws down the rest of his scotch and soda. "You wanna come back to my place?"

Justin nods. "I'd imagine that's where the breeches are, yeah."

They grab an Uber, deal with the are-you-clean-I'm-clean on the way, and at his apartment, Quinn settles Justin on his red velvet sectional with a drink while he heads upstairs to change. He pulls out a pair of tan riding breeches, adds a belt just in case this one decides to have fun with it, and draws on his high boots. He doesn't bother with a shirt. From long practice, Quinn knows he can yank his breeches low without removing them and still spread his legs wide. Thinking about getting fucked in the ass, he immediately hardens, and his boots clank on the industrial metal steps as he makes his way back to the living area.

"Look. At. You," Justin says, his tight jeans and ripped black shirt a stark contrast to Quinn's outfit. "Look at that big cock you've got for me." He steps up to Quinn and palms him with no preliminaries. Quinn prefers it that way. Justin strokes, and Quinn grinds shamelessly against his hand. "You like that, pretty little twink? Down on your fucking knees."

Quinn's knees hit the ground.

"Rub that thick cock while you suck mine. Get me hard to fuck you. Bet you've got a tight ass for me." Justin unzips and takes himself out: medium-sized, but stiff. Quinn can deep-throat him, no problem, and does so immediately. Justin moans. He pulls Quinn's long hair. "That's it, baby. Suck it for me. I wanna see you playing with that big cock under those breeches."

Quinn sucks him for a few minutes, the way he sucks every guy he brings home. He has a method: lips tight, plenty of tongue, suck the head hard, flutter his tongue on the underside. Jack it. Stroke balls if they're out of the pants and ignore them if they aren't. By then, Quinn's figured out what the guy likes and keeps doing it. Finally, Justin tells Quinn to drop his pants. "Condoms and lube in the drawer over there," Quinn indicates, undoing his belt, yanking his breeches to his ankles, and getting up on all fours. The soft, fuzzy shag rug thrown in front of the sectional is no accident; it's easy on the knees.

Justin goes gentler than most. He doesn't skimp on the lube, thank god, but circles Quinn and opens him a little before he slides a finger inside. He works at Quinn's ass, then slips in another. Quinn leans back into it and begs. *More more more, I love your fingers in me, gimme another, love it, want you to fuck me soon, gimme more, fuck me with your fingers* — A third slides into him. *Fuck me. Fuck me harder with them. Open me up for your dick. Fuck me with your cock.*

Justin pushes his pants down and rolls on a condom. Quinn feels the familiar stretching, his tight ring expanding, opening, the usual feeling of his muscles forced. It hurts, then it doesn't, then it hurts again, but it feels good at the same time, and Justin doesn't hurt bad because his cock isn't that big. He settles in and hits that spot that makes Quinn cry out with pleasure. *Fuck me. Do it now. I'll be such a good boy if you fuck me. Please fuck me hard. Fuck me, I want your dick, your dick feels so good in my ass, I'm so full oh god I'm so full, fuck me* — Justin pumps at him, thrusting hard, gripping Quinn by his narrow hips. Quinn arches into him like a cat stretching, but too soon, Justin shudders, jerks, and it ends.

He slides out, stands up, and starts dressing.

"You're a good fuck," Justin says. "Tight little ass. Cute too."

Quinn realizes Justin won't be getting him off. What a motherfucker.

He flips Quinn's hair — Quinn bats him away. Fucker can't

manage to get him off, fucker can't touch his hair. "See you around?" Justin says, before his pants are up. "Anytime you want to ... "

"I didn't get off — you don't get it again," Quinn says. "See you." He summarily kicks Justin out, goes up to his room, pulls his boots off, drops his breeches on the floor, and steps into his enormous shower. Quinn likes the water skin-scaldingly hot after one of these nights, telling himself he needs to wash the cigarette smoke out of his hair. He really wants to scrub the guys off his skin; to wash their touch down the drain. It always feels good... until it doesn't, when everything pivots from that blissful blankness into the misery of memory.

Somehow his cock's still hard, goddammit. Quinn takes it in hand and jacks it the way he likes: he plays with the underside, then jerks slowly; pauses, plays with the same spot, then jerks it again, faster and faster. Quinn thinks about getting fucked on his back, his cock slipping against some bigger man's stomach. That bigger man's pinning Quinn down and telling him what a good boy he is, such a good boy to get fucked, what a tight ass — he needs to take his whole cock, yes he does, good boys take the whole thing — Quinn spills fast after that, then scrubs himself all over, hard, head to toe, and lets the soap run off him. He stands in the scalding water for a long time.

Quinn sets the coffeemaker, programs the alarms, and passes the fuck out. Holding his bear, he closes his eyes and sees a deep pool, light bouncing off the sides, glittering and refracting, and him all alone at the bottom.

* * *

The Savannah Hunt Club starts cub-hunting early, in the beginning of August. Everyone shows up to ride across the countryside at a leisurely pace as Henry's brother Alexander and those bastards whip the new pups into shape. Not like they're training them to kill the fox or anything; that would be totally barbaric. They just chase them around. Everyone would be mortified and appalled if they actually killed one. Dark-haired, linebacker-looking Henry Culliver appears on his enormous horse. He always does. Lucky and Thor Jasper don't have a damn thing to do, so they come as well, unruly brown curls sticking out from under their helmets. Quinn chugs both brandy and coffee in equal amounts to try to wake the fuck up as his groom hands him his hunter, a blood bay named Mister. Quinn and Henry ride near the front of the group, fussily known as the field. The Jasper twins skulk near the back. They'd rather trot around and swig brandy than take fences. The August heat hasn't dropped down yet, and the mist hasn't quite burned off. You could almost believe in a morning like this, if you were the type of person who believed in mornings.

Quinn makes his latest lay sound funny and stupid. Henry laughs and agrees he was a dick. They separate when Henry's Hector shies away from a fence. Hector acts like a bitch that way sometimes, but Henry always sticks his seat, something Quinn has admired since they were kids. He doesn't know if he's ever seen Henry fall off a horse, not even a snotty little pony. Quinn's close up to the hounds, standing still during a check (the stupid-ass name they use for a rest when the hounds have lost the fox's scent), when he notices a tall man atop a gray horse lazing on a loose rein. The man has long, straight brown hair ponytailed behind a fashionable helmet and proper form atop his immaculate and expensive tack.

The man gives Quinn the familiar up-and-down. Quinn lowers his eyes and looks sweet and innocent as possible: the man might be good for a quick fuck. Luckily, no one's asked Quinn if he's ever had a real boyfriend. He keeps waiting, but the question never comes. The closest he ever came was his best friend Calhoun, and they were never a romantic thing, just besties-who-fucked-around, but they could suck each other off *and* trust one another. That should count for something if anything does, but Savannah makes assumptions and Quinn just lets her have them.

Now Calhoun has some amazingly hot boyfriend from Charleston who adores the ground he walks on. Quinn sticks to fast fucks from Club Metro. When Henry asks him about it, he laughs and says it's easier and less messy that way, then he regales Henry with tales of his latest hookup. Henry always laughs. Quinn Rutledge learned a long time ago to make things funny that aren't funny at all. He also learned that when you do, people laugh along with you and stop asking questions. You can throw things out to the world and hold them close at the same time. People want to believe a smile.

Quinn keeps the long-haired man in mind. But no talking during checks, especially this close to the hounds. So he keeps his eyes forward, lowered, looking as submissive and sweet as possible.

They finally trot off. Quinn stays close to the man, who eventually turns to him. "You ride well."

"Equestrian studies at Savannah School of Art," Quinn explains.

"Ah," the man says. "You'd have to, then. Elliston Ashford. Ellis. I grew up here and recently moved back. My mother still lives here."

"Quinn Rutledge. Nice to meet you." He smirks a little. He thinks he can get away with it after the up-and-down, and it'll probably help him get laid. "Sir."

"Cheeky."

"I'm only being polite to my elders."

"You're being bratty and we both know it."

"Am I now?" Quinn asks as they trot along a berm between old rice paddies. Mister keeps stride with Ellis's gray horse, and he and Ellis post up and down, up and down at the same time.

Ellis rolls his eyes. "How old are you?"

"Old enough to consent."

"Aren't we forward?"

"I caught your once-over during the check."

"Guilty."

"So what do you do? Sir?" Quinn asks, just to needle him.

"Architecture, brat, and you do ride well, Quinn."

"Thank you." They chat about their horses for a while, then settle into the who-knows-who, who's-related-to-who on which greater Savannah turns. They aren't cousins — miracle of miracles — and Ellis is too old to have gone to school with the older brothers or sisters of anyone that Quinn knows. His parents don't know Quinn's parents; his mother's name doesn't sound familiar, and neither does his father's, who Ellis says — in a tone that makes it clear he won't discuss it further — "has passed." When the hunt ends, Henry still hasn't caught up. Ellis offers Quinn some of his brandy, which he doesn't seem to take more than a small sip of. "Thanks," Quinn says, and takes a hefty swig. "The good stuff," he comments.

"No sense in bringing anything else." Ellis dismounts. "Would you like to meet me for dinner sometime, Quinn?"

Quinn blinks. He doesn't think anyone's ever asked him to dinner and now he can't help but stop and try to remember if that's true. By now, Henry has caught up and he stands behind Ellis, still mounted. "SAY YES," Henry mouths.

"Sure." Quinn shrugs, snapping out of it. "Why not?"

"You sure?" Ellis asks. "Took you awhile."

"Yeah," Quinn says, like it doesn't matter at all. "I'll do dinner."

Ellis takes his phone from the case attached to his saddle and hands it to Quinn. "Text yourself," he says. Quinn does as he asks. "Give you a call?" Ellis says. "Say, tonight, if you're not busy?"

Quinn shrugs again, bodily shorthand for "I don't care." He's long perfected that look, coming out at sixteen in a prep school where most students believed in The Gay Agenda. Ellis takes his helmet off, unties his hair, and shakes it out. Oh god, that long, gorgeous hair, down past his shoulders, a light brown, naturally streaked blonde. Quinn dismounts, unsnaps his own helmet, and pulls his shoulder-length hair out of its tie in all its perfection: shiny, straight to his shoulders with no crimp from the ponytail holder. God, it took him forever to find a tie that wouldn't leave a mark. Ellis stares. *Totally getting fucked tonight. Dinner, and then fucked.*

Quinn thinks about it all day, this man with the long hair taking him to dinner then back to his place. Probably a nice place, too: Ellis clearly has money, family or otherwise, and will have accumulated some decent possessions at his age. Even better, it'll be nice for once to get fucked by someone who, at his age, knows how to do it, and do it well.

The text comes around three. *Drinks at The Low Man and then dinner at Oliver?*

What time?

7 ok with you?

7's great.

Quinn agonizes over his clothes. He almost calls Henry or his best friend, Calhoun for help. In the end he decides to go total frat boy—Ellis seems like he'll appreciate the type. Quinn picks a baby-blue checked button down to match his eyes, a pair of khaki shorts, easily yanked down, and sandals, but nice ones. When he walks into The Low Man at 7:15, fashionably late, he sees Ellis lounging in the low-lit bar wearing a gray linen suit with a dark green bow tie. He has a full tumbler of something in front of him that appears untouched. Fuck him. Ellis looks Quinn up and down in the half-dark.

"Cute," he comments.

"Thanks," Quinn says dryly. "I was unaware we were dressing for dinner."

"I always dress for dinner."

"Sorry about that." Quinn hops onto a leather barstool and twirls a little. "What're you drinking?"

Ellis holds up a hand. "I should make you go home and change."

"*Excuse me*?"

"I should make you go home and change. You'll look adorable in a suit, and I won't look like I'm robbing the cradle. But I didn't warn you to dress for dinner. Next time."

The realization comes slowly. "You're not fucking with me."

"No. I most emphatically am not."

Mother. Fucker. "You would send me home to change?"

"If I'd already asked you to wear a suit and you showed up in this? Yes."

"Then fuck you, if it's that goddamn important, I'll go home and change so we're matchy-matchy."

"I would be grateful, Quinn. But hurry up, I'm hungry."

Quinn's pissed, but a tiny part of him's turned on. He loves when someone orders him around, preferably an older someone. So he leaves the bar, calls *another* Uber, and makes it wait while he goes inside and changes quickly into his favorite seersucker suit, a bowtie with tiny pink flowers and pink striped socks, topped by white bucks. Plus a white and pink belt. Summer in Savannah, what the fuck. When else can you get away with it?

Forty-five minutes later, he arrives back at The Low Man. Ellis scrutinizes him. "Much better," he says. "Seersucker suits you. And white bucks too. Maybe you're not an irredeemable savage. Better worn during the day, but we'll let it slide for now. What are you drinking, Quinn?"

"Scotch and soda." He twirls on the stool again. Ellis grabs it, stops him, and glares.

Ellis hails the bartender and orders for him, which annoys Quinn. He can order for himself. Only fucking girls let a man order for them, and he tells Ellis so.

Ellis gives him a half-smile. "Uh-huh."

"The fuck's that mean?"

"You need to get over your constant use of the word 'fuck,'" Ellis comments. He brushes some of that gorgeous brown hair behind an ear and sips at his drink.

"But it's such a wonderful word," Quinn says as sweetly as possible. "It's a verb, a noun, an adjective, an adverb, an interjection, an exclamation—"

"And it's only effective when used judiciously."

"You're kind of a dick," Quinn says bluntly. "You made me go home and change and now you're harassing me about my language like I'm a ten-year-old."

"Mmmm," Ellis says noncommittally. "I suggested you change. You're the one who did it."

This is becoming tiresome just to get what he could have by walking into Club Metro and hanging out on a barstool for ten minutes — with eyeliner, more comfortable clothes, and maybe a bump or two of coke. "Explain why I shouldn't tell you to fuck off and walk out right now," Quinn says.

"You're a smart-mouthed brat," Ellis says. "I'm the one who should walk out. I don't know why I'm bothering to stay, except you're adorable, I like a smart mouth, and I like a good little submissive."

"I never said I always bottomed!" Quinn protests. His voice rises but fuck all who hears him. They'll all be talking about who he went out with anyway. If two Savannahians meet in a bar, they buy some drinks, loosen some tongues, and walk out with gossip. Standard operating procedure in the prettiest city in the world.

Ellis snorts. "Have you *ever* fucked another man? I mean, have you ever been the one actually doing the fucking?"

Quinn knows he's reddening and can't stop himself.

"Mm-hmm. That's what I thought, pretty boy. You like it on the bottom. You also desperately need civilizing. Fucking savage."

"I thought you weren't supposed to use the word 'fuck,'" Quinn says smugly. "Sir."

"Judiciously, brat. Judiciously. Finish your drink so I can take you to dinner and probably complain about your manners." Either Ellis has ordered another or he hasn't touched his. And he leaves a full glass of whatever when they walk out. Weird.

Quinn rolls his eyes — he was raised in upper crust Savannah. He knows how to behave at a table, and Ellis doesn't find a single thing to bitch about. "Should've known a rich boy would eat like a civilized human," he says as they finish their steak. Quinn's almost squirming. He knows what's coming next and it should be mind-blowing. Ellis will have him on his knees and begging. They've spent dinner talking local politics; school (Ellis went to Thurston Prep and St. Albert's as well, just many classes ahead of Quinn, then Emory and Duke), what Quinn expects to do with his degree (probably equine journalism); what type of music they like (Ellis prefers old REM and U2; Quinn likes David Bowie, Queen, and Johnny Cash — they have a good laugh about how someone would expect the opposite of them).

"I had a nice night, Quinn," Ellis says finally. "I'd like to do it again sometime. You're adorable and fun and I enjoyed your company."

Quinn can't keep the confusion off his face. "You want to come back to my place? Coffee or a drink or anything?" Fucking? You want to come back to my place for fucking?

"You're also impatient and need to learn self-control."

"*Excuse me*?!" Quinn demands for the second time that night.

"You're adorable. Truly. I'd love to have you on your knees. Don't worry. I will, if you're patient. You're used to getting what you want and walking away from it. Instant gratification isn't good for anyone. Good night. I'll call you." Ellis picks up the bill and walks out, leaving Quinn, jaw dropped, alone at a table in Oliver.

That complete motherfucker.

Quinn goes home and jerks off to Ellis fucking him in the ass while he begs and tells him he'll be a good boy, he swears he'll be so good, look how good he's being. Then he takes another scalding hot shower. Should've known. The only guy he *hasn't* met at a club in god knows how long and he refuses to fuck him. Of course. Quinn should've known that it never works out for him. Too much of a brat. Too used to getting what he wants. Wrong clothes, wrong attitude, wrong everything. He stands in the shower and scrubs and scrubs. Afterwards, Quinn curls up in bed. It flits across his mind, the way it always does when things get bad: the time he nearly drowned when he was two. The usual story: a party, everyone thinks someone else is watching the baby and no one's paying attention, not really. Quinn remembers kneeling to look at the light fracturing, spider-webbing across the pool at night. And he was falling, down, down, headfirst, then a gentle flip to his back. He could see the people as faraway blurs, smears, the water around him so clear, the breath he took so easy, but heavy and strange. Quinn remembers staring, staring up, the water fracturing around him, the slow, slow movement of his limbs, wanting so badly to close his eyes.

He didn't choke until they brought him up; until he tried to breathe the air again, until he tried to scream, lungs full, suddenly terrified, suddenly aware of how alone he'd been down in the water; alone with all that dancing light, the people far, far away, not missing him, not caring, not noticing the baby in the bottom of the pool. He falls asleep and dreams of water.

So when Ellis calls the next day, he doesn't pick up.

Nor does he pick up the call later that afternoon.

Or the next day.

Or the day after that.

Motherfucker's persistent, though. He keeps calling. Quinn ignores him.

Quinn goes cub-hunting again later in the week. Henry, Wills, and their brother Alexander have gone back to school; the Jasper twins show up, so he rides with Lucky and Thor. They stick to the back of the pack, but eventually, inexorably, Quinn draws ahead until he's riding near the hounds again. He likes to take the jumps too much. Savannah's given them another gorgeous morning, a little hotter, but with the same lingering mist, the same promising glow.

The sunlight's shifting from gold to yellow when he sees Ellis at a check. Quinn glances up, then looks away.

Ellis doesn't speak, perfectly proper, until they trot off. He pulls his gray horse next to Quinn's Mister. "You didn't have to ignore all my calls."

"You didn't have to refuse to go home with me," Quinn retorts. "Don't know if you're aware, but that's generally how a date ends when you find the other person acceptable."

"You're savage." Ellis sighs.

"You keep saying that. And yet I manage quite well for myself, thanks."

"You spent last semester nearly failing out of SASA, you spend your weekends fucking random guys you meet at Club Metro. Your parents used all their energy on your older siblings and by the time the Rutledge oops baby arrived there wasn't much left for you. You're on a road to nowhere, brat. Even your cousin Delia thinks so, and she's got her head on straighter than just about any Rutledge in the city."

"What the fuck?" Quinn demands.

Ellis shrugs. "Savannah likes to talk. Savannah especially likes to talk when you buy it liquor."

"So what's your goddamn point?" Ellis has hit him hard, ugly, and it hurts more than Quinn wants to admit, even to himself. Knowing Delia thinks he's a fuckup might be the worst. His cousin has shared the same class with him since kindergarten. He loves her like a sister. "You don't want to fuck me, so why do you keep calling?"

"Not interested in fucking you currently, no. In civilizing you *before* I fuck you? Yes. I believe it's called an actual relationship."

Quinn snorts. "Uh-huh. Right. Like I'm going to believe that." Like hell Ellis wants an actual *relationship*. He doesn't know what the *fuck* Ellis wants, but he wants something. However, Quinn doesn't need any part of someone who informs him that Delia, of all people, thinks he's a fuckup. *Thanks for reminding me how much I suck, asshole. See you later.*

"Too bad for you. Because you need someone to look out for you."

"I think I'm doing a fine job on my own."

Quinn rides back to the Jasper twins. They probably have plenty of brandy left. In Savannah, it's never too early for day drinking.

But something nags at him.

Ellis is right.

CHAPTER 2

Ellis doesn't know why the fuck he wants to deal with this mouthy brat who seems to care about nothing other than having fun and turning another trick. Unfortunately, he has a soft spot for lost souls; especially when lost souls come with asses like Quinn's, smart mouths demanding to get shut, big blue eyes, and mile-wide submissive streaks. He's beautiful. He's fun and he's smart and there's a core of sweetness there, once you get past the snark. Ellis is falling already, and falling hard.

Quinn can ride, which attracted Ellis from the beginning. Then seeing his outrage when Ellis told him to go change — oh Christ, his cock had risen under the bar. What a brat. Ellis could change that. Quinn didn't pick up Ellis's phone calls as punishment for not taking him home and fucking him. Quinn wanted it, and wanted it bad; he kept biting his lip and shifting all through dinner. Ellis wanted so much to reach over and palm him, to see how much his cock had tented out that seersucker. God, his cock: Ellis could see it in those tight breeches, big and thick. Ellis loves a big cock on a little twink like Quinn, something so dirty about a big dick on such a delicate frame. And they'd *invented* the word twink for Quinn, with that naturally pale blond hair and those big eyes, his pouty lips, slim but muscled body, and from what Ellis has seen of his arms, probably a totally smooth chest.

But Ellis had asked around. He always asks around, especially with a brat like this. He made that mistake once, not asking. Ellis tries hard to only make the same mistake once.

And it's dangerous, but he knows he's already gone for Quinn. Ellis falls, and he falls hard. It's part of who he is. He knows it, and he also knows there isn't much he can do about it but deal with the inevitable broken heart. He treads as carefully as he can, but it happens over and over, these beautiful boys who work their way into his life and walk out again. They do it as easily as shutting a door, as simply as saying goodbye. They toss it off, they wander off into the world, leaving Ellis with empty hands, with an empty, echoing house. He tries so hard, but still, they always go.

But Quinn: those smart remarks from those pouty lips, Christ. Ellis wants those lips wrapped around his dick sooner rather than later, but he has to be patient with Quinn, something about his eyes, about the way he looks at Ellis. Quinn's mouthy; he's touchy for some reason Ellis can't put his finger on. But he will. He'll find out.

So Ellis had asked around. Savannah loves a good gossip, if you know who to ask. And Ellis knows who to ask. A week later he has his answers. Quinn is failing out of SASA, mainly due to absences: he just needs to get his sweet little ass into the classroom. He fucks too many guys — easy to find out; ask the bouncers at the best club in the city and they'll tell you he leaves with a different one every weekend. Some drug use but no real addiction. He scored some time with Quinn's cousin Delia by claiming to be a boyfriend of Quinn's who felt pretty worried about him, could they talk? Delia apparently loves Quinn like her own self and sat down with him at a bar for an hour and a half. He got her trashed and everything spilled out. Then he called her an Uber and put her in it. No one drives drunk on Ellis's watch.

Then when Ellis wouldn't fuck him, the brat wouldn't take his calls. Ellis had sighed, kind of figured him for finished, until Quinn saw him again out hunting. He thought maybe he'd give him another try. So after Quinn trots back to whomever he'd been riding with, Ellis decides on a plan. He waits until the early afternoon, when he takes a break from drafting, goes out to the balcony in the office (nothing like a posh office), and gives Quinn one more phone call.

Quinn picks up this time.

"You ready to try dinner again?" he asks.

"You ready to take me home this time?"

"No."

"Maybe find another dinner partner."

"Maybe I like this one."

Silence.

"Mmm-hmm. Maybe I'll pick you up at eight. Maybe you'll be dressed like a human being this time, rather than a frat boy," Ellis says. He likes a man to dress for dinner. It feels more civilized. Plus he doesn't feel like he's robbing the fucking cradle.

"Sure. Fine. You want me to text you my address, or you get that information off the greater Savannah gossip circuit too?"

"I'd appreciate a text. Eight o'clock. I'll call you when I get there."

The text comes through a minute later.

Quinn wears a linen suit this time. It's bespoke, goddamn this boy has money, and a nice apartment too. "Where are we headed?" Quinn asks sweetly as he slides into the front of Ellis's black Mercedes. Ellis glares at him pointedly, and doesn't take the car out of park until Quinn buckles his seatbelt. "Sorry," Quinn says, and lowers his eyes.

So he's going to try to play it that way. Fuck. This'll be a hell of a lot harder to resist than the smart mouth. Ellis loves a sweet little submissive. Quinn acting the sweet boy for *him* —

Ellis shoves it down. He tries so hard to keep that tamped down, to stuff it somewhere else, to leave it alone. He knows what they call what he wants, and it's not ... okay.

"I thought we might hit up Loki," Ellis says. "The duck confit nachos are spectacular."

"I'd like that," Quinn says. "If this is a date, do I get to hold your hand?"

"No," Ellis says without thinking. He doesn't want to give in to the innocent act, for his own sake, and he wants to teach Quinn not to manipulate him.

Quinn looks crestfallen. Ellis can't tell if he's faking it or not. So when he tosses his keys to the valet, he picks up Quinn's hand. "Changed my mind," he says briskly. "I'd rather everyone know you're with me."

When he glances over, he sees Quinn smiling a little. Not a lot, but a little bit, and to himself. He doesn't seem to realize Ellis is looking.

They get a good table, one in the back, darkish and against the wall. No one else around, and they can speak without being overheard. Quinn doesn't talk much. He keeps his eyes down. Ellis's dick stiffens under the table. Fuck, but he looks adorable this way, so sweet, lips pouted out, ready to do what someone (Ellis) tells him to. "What's with the innocent act?" Ellis finally asks, after several attempts at conversation veer off into nowhere.

"What d'you mean?" Quinn looks up without raising his chin. Fuck. Everything. Jesus god. He even holds his hands folded nicely in his lap, on top of his napkin. And that three-piece linen suit does look delicious on him; he's wearing a lavender and white flowered tie. When he looks up, Ellis can see how big his eyes look. They change color, he's noticed; the lavender turns them a beautiful gray.

"You know exactly what I'm talking about. Don't play dumb with me." If Ellis acts aggressive, if he pushes, he can break through this and relieve the tension that's murdering him right now. He grits his teeth and leans his elbows on the dark wooden table.

"I don't know what you mean, though."

"Except you do."

"No, I really don't." Quinn blinks innocently, baby deer eyes. Christ Almighty. His hands stay folded. A little angel, so well-behaved, so sweet, so ready to do whatever Ellis wants. He senses

Quinn likes the game as much as he does, and the idea hardens him further. Sweet Christ, this boy is killing him. He's falling harder. He wants to take Quinn home, put him on the couch, feed him, cuddle him, take him upstairs, and fuck him. Then cuddle him to sleep. Just the *idea* of it all, of holding Quinn and kissing him and fucking him — Ellis *will* be jerking off tonight.

"Where'd that smart mouth go? What's with the lowered eyes and the sweetness, huh? You think that's gonna trick me into fucking you? Tell me what you want to eat."

Quinn asks for a truly enormous amount of food — oh well, he *is* in his teens — and when the waiter appears, Ellis orders for them. Quinn doesn't bitch or moan. "Didn't that piss you off, that I ordered for you like a girl?" Ellis taunts him.

"No," Quinn says. But Ellis sees his jaw grind, just a little. Ellis smirks. He only has to keep pushing; Quinn'll drop that innocent bit and the brat'll come back. Nice to know he *can* behave if he wants to, though. That knowledge makes Ellis's dick stiffer and he pushes it to the side.

"You're not sweet and innocent. You're a brat. You're just pretending because you think it'll get my dick in your ass tonight." He's intentionally vulgar, seeing if it'll elicit a reaction. But Quinn isn't the only one who wants that. God, he'd be so good to have pinned to the bed and begging for it. Such a delicate frame, he's probably *tight*, no matter how much fucking he's done.

Quinn keeps his eyes down.

"You are going to wait," Ellis tells him. If he tells Quinn this, he tells himself the same thing. But he allows himself to trace his thumb along Quinn's lips, uncertain by now which of them he's tormenting. "And you are going to wait. I know you can fix your life up. I believe you can fix your life up, Q. And we can wait until you do it."

"What the fuck are you talking about?" Quinn finally bursts out. The innocent act drops suddenly, almost violently. His face changes from lowered eyes to angry, narrowed ones; his mouth shifts from a slight smile to a tight twist. His brow furrows and he pushes his blond hair out of his face.

"Stop failing out of SASA."

"How —"

"Get rid of the coke in your pocket." That's a wild guess.

"What the *fuck*?" But a good one, apparently.

"Stop picking up random guys. Every goddamn weekend, Quinn? Really?"

"I don't —" Now he's going to lie about it. Even worse. Ellis's stomach flips.

"You do. Act like a normal human. Dress for dinner. Stop saying 'fuck' all the damn time."

"But —"

"Act as smart as we both know you are. You got into SASA, for god's sake. You're no idiot. Oh, and I expect to see your pretty face out cub-hunting *every* morning. The hounds go out, you go out. You need to learn to wake up instead of partying."

"I'm sorry, have you mistaken me for Eliza fucking Doolittle?" Quinn snaps.

"See? *My Fair Lady* reference. You *are* smart." Ellis can snark with the best of them, and Quinn's about to see it.

"And why the hell are you doing this?" Quinn demands. "What the fuck do you get out of it? Some kind of weird kink?"

Ellis ignores the kink comment. He's not discussing that. He does his best to ignore it and so far he's been successful. Ellis has managed to always push the impulse off onto something else, something more — acceptable. He knows what they call the thing he thinks about all the time, and it's not something you talk about in polite company. "No kink. Savior complex."

Their nachos arrive, the perfect moment, and they both quiet for a second. Ellis picks one up, blows on it so it's cool, and holds it out to Quinn. Quinn takes it delicately from Ellis's hand, a gentle crunch, so sensual without either lips or tongue touching him. Ellis immediately hardens again. Quinn's wide eyes tell him no one's ever done that for him before, that he wants more. "You liked that," Ellis says, letting his voice go silky. "You liked that a lot. You want that all the time, honey? You like to have someone take care of you. That's all you want. You want someone to fuck you and pet you afterwards, Quinn. I just told you what you have to do to get it."

"But what if I can't —"

"You can. Your cock's hard enough to pound nails right now, by the way."

"How the fuck do you know?" the brat roaring right back when Ellis pushes too hard.

"Lucky guess," Ellis says. Because he knows *he's* certainly stiff, thinking about Quinn in his bed to play with all night and then cuddle and fuss over. "If you'd done all those things I just told you to do, I'd take you home, play with you until you were exhausted, tell you how good you were, tuck you into bed with me, and cuddle you until you fell asleep. You'd love that, wouldn't you? You want me to hold your cock while you drift off? I can do that, too." He leans over and lets his hot breath tickle Quinn's ear. "You know you'd love every second of it. On your knees. Getting fucked. I'd always make sure you got off, unless you were *very* bad, and I'd never, ever do anything you didn't want me to. You'd be completely safe, honey. You've been waiting for this your whole goddamn life."

Quinn bites his lip and shifts in his chair. His eyes drop again.

Quinn would never know it, but he certainly has Ellis. Ellis's craving this. He wants Quinn approximately sometime yesterday, sweet and well-behaved for *him*, good for *him*. He wants to tell him what a sweet boy he is and take care of him. It's so fucked up. Ellis tries hard not to care how fucked up. He wants to cuddle Quinn to death. He wants to fuck him. He wants Quinn, most of all, to need him, to reach for him in the night, to want him in return. He wants it so much it almost chokes him.

"I don't even know where to *start*," Quinn says. Ellis catches the despair in his voice and almost needs to swoop in and cuddle him. He wants to assure Quinn he's smart and capable and that he can do this, he really can. Ellis will help him.

"Get rid of the coke. Start there," Ellis tells him, only a little bit away from his Dom voice. "Now."

Quinn stands and returns a minute or so later. "Gone," he says.

"What'd you do with it?"

"I flushed several grams of good coke, Ellis, god," Quinn snaps. Ellis doesn't miss the use of his actual name. The first time: it means something. Quinn's made a choice.

"Now you wake up and go cub-hunting with me in the morning. Call your groom. Tell him to meet you at the kennels at seven."

Quinn groans. "Seriously?" His head drops against the back of the chair. "I have to wake up at *five* to go cubbing at seven. Do you know how much it sucks to wake up at five?"

"Yes. And you wake up every morning after this. You need to learn to get up in the morning. It keeps you out of trouble at night."

Quinn sighs. He picks up his phone and makes the call.

Ellis's proud. Quinn really wants this; Quinn wants cuddled and taken care of. Which is all Ellis wants: to cuddle Quinn and take care of him. After he fucks the hell out of him, preferably pinned down. That pretty little face looking up at him, that sweet little ass wiggling on his hard cock. Fingering him open. God, Ellis loves fingering a begging little twink.

"You've been very good tonight," Ellis says after Quinn hangs up. He bites back *a very good boy.* That's what he really, really wants to tell Quinn: *you've been a very good boy. Such a very, very good boy for me, Quinn. Tell me what you want now, and I'll give it to you, honey.*

"Then why do I feel like I just signed my goddamn life away?" Quinn asks.

"Because you're used to one kind of life, which you think is the only possible way to live, and I'm about to show you a much better one. One you've never experienced; one you don't understand, is far superior."

"Ellis?" he says. His voice teeters a little, something in it Ellis has never heard.

Ellis has no idea what Quinn wants to say.

"I'm kind of scared."

It may be the first honest thing Quinn's ever said to him. That, and the look he threw about wanting to hold Ellis's hand, but Ellis isn't quite sure about that.

"You'd be stupid if you weren't," Ellis tells him. "Change is always frightening."

"You're like, basically forcing me to grow up all at once," he says. Quinn looks down and twists the black linen napkin in his lap. Totally adorable.

"No. I'm asking you to take control of your life. Those are two different things," Ellis says gently. He lets himself stroke Quinn's face. Quinn looks up at him. Ellis can read so many things in that look at once: fear and hope and desperation and despair. He hesitates. Maybe he's pushed Quinn too far, asked for too much.

Once they've finished eating, Ellis pays the bill and takes Quinn's hand. "C'mon," he says. "You can stay at my place tonight. No hooking up. No cuddling, because we know where that'll lead and neither of us can resist that. But you can stay. Okay? I'll take you to your place in the morning to get your riding clothes."

Quinn nods.

"I will rub your back though."

"Okay," Quinn says.

"You can even jack off if you need to after that." Ellis hesitates a second. What the fuck, it can't hurt. "But I'd like to watch."

"Seriously?" Quinn asks. Ellis glances down. Quinn's already risen, sitting in the black leather seat of the Mercedes. Oh god, he tents out that linen suit, his cock so big on that delicate frame. Ellis wants so much to play with it.

"Seriously." Ellis shouldn't. He knows he shouldn't. But he wants it so much and really, this is such a small thing compared to what he really, really wants.

Ellis knows he has good taste. His house looks immaculate: a restored antebellum, small but beautiful, all the original cypress flooring. He had bookshelves built in and filled them with curios; the furniture veers towards overstuffed and comfortable. He takes Quinn to the master bedroom, a haven of plush white down, everything fluffy and made for comfort. "You can take off everything but your underwear," he says sternly. "Leave those on. There are hangers in the closet for your suit." Ellis does his best not to look while Quinn strips but he can't help himself. All that lean muscle, god. "Lie down on the bed on your stomach," he orders, not quite in his Dom voice, but just a little bit deeper. He can't help curbing that voice with Quinn up here, Quinn mostly naked, Quinn in his bed. Quinn obediently moves the covers down and lies on his belly, his adorable little ass in the air, covered in black briefs. Ellis's a sucker for briefs. They hold everything *right there*, tight and neat. And oh Christ does he look good, long, lean arms folded under his head, the smooth planes of his back exposed, curving up to that perfect ass, so small and grabbable, the long thighs, slightly spread. Oh god. Ellis wants so much to slip a finger between those legs and feel for what he's sure is a tight, pink little pucker.

But he straddles Quinn and starts work on his back. Quinn's back feels knotted, tense, as if he thinks he may need to run from something. "What's wrong?" Ellis asks. Because with a back like that, it must be something. You don't feel this way unless there's something.

"I don't know," Quinn mutters. He means *I don't want to tell you*, sure as if he's said the words. Ellis can't help but feel a stab of disappointment. He knows Quinn doesn't trust him yet. But he wants him to, god does he want him to. He wants to hold Quinn; he wants Quinn to trust him with all his secrets. Not because he needs to know them: because Quinn needs to tell them.

"You do know what's wrong," Ellis says gently. "Tell me. Let me help."

"'M scared." This is a big admission on Quinn's end and Ellis knows it. He runs his fingers through Quinn's gorgeous hair.

"Of what?" Ellis makes his voice soft and caring.

"That I'm making a huge mistake." Another big admission, more honesty.

"Quinn," Ellis says gently, "you can always walk away. No one's keeping you here. No one's making you be here."

"Except what if I fall in love with you and I don't wanna

leave?" he asks all in a rush. Ellis can hear the end of that sure as if Quinn had spoken it: *and you make me leave anyway.*

Ellis can't help himself. He leans down and kisses the back of Quinn's neck. Quinn'll feel his hard-on, but too goddamn bad. "You can always leave," he says again. "But as long as you keep trying, no matter how much you mess up, I would never ask you to." His voice almost catches. That happened with Mark, with Logan, with so many of those beautiful, beautiful boys. He'd tried so hard with Mark, especially. Ellis had held him through his withdrawals. He'd gotten him counseling. He'd taken care of Mark, he'd taken such good care of Mark and he couldn't help him in the end. Last Ellis had heard he was using again. Ellis had told Mark he would never have to leave as long as he kept trying. Mark had decided it wasn't worth trying anymore. Of all of them, Mark may have hurt Ellis the worst, because Mark's pain came from a deep well of hopelessness Ellis could never touch.

Ellis had only wanted to help. He'd never done a goddamn thing with Mark. Not once. Never more than kissed his forehead.

His mother hates all this. "Why do you find these kids and pour your heart and soul into them?" she always demands. She hates that he's gay and hates that he likes younger men even more; she loves to pull out the "This would have killed your father" line. "You just break your own goddamn heart, Elliston." Then she pauses. And the inevitable comes. "You know it would have destroyed your father." His father, his father. Jesus fucking Christ. Let's not talk about Dad, who despite his alcoholism didn't give a flying fuck that his son liked men. Unlike Mummy.

Ellis doesn't want to explain it: the thing he tries so hard not to think about, the one he shoves down and ignores, except while he's jerking off. "You have a fucking savior complex," his friend Terrance said once. "You gotta quit this shit."

Ellis had just shrugged.

Really, Ellis probably just wishes someone had saved *him* when he'd needed it, when he'd spent all his time in clubs, fucking random guys, snorting lines, almost failing out of school after his father had died rear-ending the truck on I-16 coming home from the bar. The only person who ever saw and accepted Ellis completely — gone. Somehow Ellis had pulled himself out of it. But if someone had come and lifted him up instead, maybe it would have been easier. Maybe it would have happened sooner. Maybe it wouldn't have wrecked him so badly. When he helps Quinn, he soothes some hurt part of himself.

Maybe, and if he's more honest with himself he knows this hits closer, Ellis needs to be needed. He craves being needed. It means he matters, it means — everything, really. It means someone wants him there. He wants Quinn to want him there. He wants Quinn to take care of. If he could take care of Quinn, love Quinn, if Quinn would let him in ...

So he uses everything he has on Quinn's back: his elbows, his forearms, his fists. Ellis unknots him, cracks his back, unsticks his muscles, unclenches his jaw and relaxes his neck. Once Quinn feels like a quivery ball of jello, Ellis asks, "Better?"

"Yeah," Quinn says. His voice sounds far away. "Will you do this all the time, if I'm good?"

"Whenever you want," Ellis says honestly. He loves feeling Quinn under him like this, making him feel good and soothing him this way.

"I'll be so good," Quinn says. "I'll be so so so good, you won't believe it. I'll be so good for you, Ellis."

Ellis laughs. "You're hard now, aren't you?" He knows *he* is, hearing Quinn say how goddamn good he'll be.

"Oh god, as a fucking rock."

"Stop saying 'fuck,'" Ellis admonishes. "I swear I'll break you of that."

"I'll try," Quinn says contritely. "I'll try so hard to be good."

Murder. Absolute murder.

"Then turn over and let me watch," Ellis says. "Take your briefs off and let me watch you."

"Do I get to watch you, too?" Quinn asks shyly. "I'd like that."

That last little bit destroys him. "Yes," Ellis says. "You can." God, thirty-seven and you'd think he'd have learned some fucking self-control by now, but those few words shatter it. "Let me get something to clean up with. You want lube?"

"Yes, please," Quinn says, eyes down. Oh *god*.

They both lie back on the pillows; Ellis will admit he's somewhat of a pillow slut and owns enough for a family of four. Quinn has taken off his briefs while Ellis went to get some washcloths and, oh god, his cock is *big*, even bigger with everything around it trimmed. He looks at Ellis with those big eyes. "Do you like it?" Quinn asks, big eyes staring up at Ellis. Ellis likes it so much he wants it in his mouth, Jesus Christ.

"What do you think, Quinn?" Ellis asks carefully.

"I think you do," Quinn says. He lowers his eyes again. "I *hope* you like it."

Ellis pulls off his own boxers. "Oh you're *big*," Quinn says. "And not just your cock, either." Ellis knows his balls are large, that they hang big and ripe between his legs. Quinn has already started toying with himself while he stares at Ellis. He's younger: he'll go quicker. Ellis watches him carefully; he'll learn how to jerk Quinn himself if he pays attention. Quinn holds his cock and rubs the underside of his head. When he slicks himself, he does it almost luxuriously, wetting every bit of his cock, rubbing lube all around his head. Then slowly, slowly Quinn strokes himself, holding himself lightly in his fist, not using nearly as much pressure as Ellis would expect. Ellis, on the other hand, uses plenty of pressure and does it fast, going all the way up and over his head each time. But Quinn keeps up those slow strokes. He arches up to his hand, stops, and rubs that spot he likes. So goddamn hot. Ellis pumps himself and watches Quinn; Quinn goes slow and watches Ellis. Pearly drops of precum appear on the tip of Quinn's cock, just a few, then more and more. He drips; he drips a *lot*. Ellis loves to watch him drip. He doesn't do it much himself, but he loves to see it in someone else. Quinn spreads the drops over his head. Finally he starts jerking himself faster. His hips thrust up into his hand. He reaches for more lube and slicks himself unbelievably, gliding his hand over himself rather than jerking. Oh god. More pearly drops appear. Quinn makes deep, contented noises in his throat.

Sweet baby Jesus, Ellis can't help himself. He reaches out and touches Quinn, who groans with pleasure and thrusts his hips at him. Ellis slides next to him. "Let me do it," he says. "Let me do it for you." He takes both their cocks in his hands and pumps them at once. They slip against his hands, against each other. Quinn just moans. Ellis can't last, especially seeing Quinn drip like this; drip onto his own cock and onto Ellis's, oh Christ. Quinn tenses and suddenly shudders hard in Ellis's hand. He shoots hot, sticky come onto them both, so much of it that Ellis loses it himself, and it mixes together — so fucking hot. Quinn bucks into his hands until he's spent. Ellis watches Quinn: his eyes squeezed shut with pleasure, his hips thrusting, head thrown back.

Finally, once he's subsided into occasional shivers, he opens his eyes and blinks sleepily. "I thought we were going to do it ourselves."

"I couldn't help it," Ellis confesses. "You were just there and you looked so good and — yeah. I shouldn't have. I told you no earlier. I'm sorry."

"No," Quinn says. "It was good. Don't apologize. I just wish you would have kissed me." He looks sulky.

"I shouldn't have done it," Ellis says: absurd, because they lie almost forehead to forehead. Quinn's breath smells improbably like candy. Ellis wants to kiss him so much. Such a small thing. He doesn't know why he stops himself, except that he has to draw a line somewhere tonight.

"I still wish you'd kiss me," Quinn sulks. "No fair getting jerked off and not kissed." He looks mad. "You say it'll be different and jerk me off anyway and still don't kiss me. I never get kissed."

"I know." And he does. You bring home guys to fuck, not kiss.

"And you put all these rules on it and you still won't —"

"I'm sorry. I shouldn't have done that. I lost control of—"

"I'm never good enough," Quinn says. He turns away, stands up, wipes himself off and pulls his briefs on. "Not ever good enough. I'm going home." He begins dressing.

"No, Quinn, that's not what I mean," Ellis says hastily. "That's not it at all. It's about —"

"I don't care what it's about. It's about how I'm not good enough. That's what it boils down to, Ellis. Not good enough. And you made me flush how many fucking grams of coke? Fuck this noise. I'm going home. Don't call me."

He walks out of Ellis's house.

Ellis knows then, that no matter what the reason, he should have kissed him.

More than that, he shouldn't have pushed Quinn so goddamn hard.

CHAPTER 3

Never good enough. Story of Quinn's fucking life. Never good enough for his family: they always called him the oops baby. Fucking Savannah calls him the Rutledge oops baby. Three older brothers, Alexander Jr., nine years older than him. His parents spent so long trying for a girl and finally got Darcy, then told everyone four kids — they were finished. Two years later, along came Quinn: the baby no one wanted and another boy, even worse. He hadn't even gotten baptized like the rest of them. They'd given away all the hand-me downs and he'd heard his mother had bitched endlessly about buying him new clothes; because Henry and Wills were so much bigger, he'd worn theirs through most of his childhood. Their mothers were always friends, and Jeannie Culliver saved everything for Quinn.

Good enough in school: Quinn was smart, smart as any of them, but no one really cared. Quinn could ride, but it was somewhere to drop him off, to keep him occupied.

Quinn has friends, but other than Calhoun, no one really close. They like him, sure, and they ask him to hang out. But no one that really — no one who really *knows* him. No one he feels like he can really talk to without joking, even Calhoun. Apparently even Delia thinks he's a fuck-up. Quinn pushes that aside or he'll start crying. He loves Delia so much.

He's Quinn Rutledge, the gay kid; Quinn Rutledge, who never shuts up; Quinn Rutledge, who Wills and Henry can just decide not to talk to for an entire goddamn year in ninth grade and no one cares, no one sticks up for him or stops them because it's Wills and Henry. Quinn Rutledge who knows all the gossip. Quinn Rutledge who says everything but who never actually says a goddamn thing at all.

He takes an Uber home. Another scalding shower, more scrubbing. He lays in bed with his battered old teddy bear. When he falls asleep, he dreams of water, water, water, the people faraway blurs, spiderwebs of light.

But he'd already set his alarm to go cubbing, so it blares at an ungodly hour. And he forgot to call the groom and tell him not to bring Mister over. Fuck all. So he has to show up. Which means he has to see Ellis. *You don't exist in my world,* he heard the famous drag queen Lady Chablis say once. You don't exist in my world. You don't exist in my world.

He chants it silently as he drives his yellow Stingray over the country roads to the kennels. As he mounts up. As Ellis rides over on Ghost. "Hey, Quinn," he says. He sounds more tentative than Quinn has ever heard him, more unsure and more worried.

"You don't exist in my world," Quinn blurts.

"Do you want some brandy?" Ellis asks, as if he hasn't spoken.

"Did I fucking stutter?" Quinn snaps. Once he's said it, he might as well not back down.

"Did I?" Ellis's voice remains mild.

"I don't want any. Neither you nor your brandy exists." Quinn turns away.

Ellis sighs. "I never said you weren't good enough."

"No, you just decided you needed to embark on some kind of fucking Eliza Doolittle project before you could deign to fuck me!" Quinn knows his voice is rising and he can't find it in himself to care. Luckily Mister stands perfectly still: good training. Quinn did it himself, not that anyone really knows or would care. "And don't think I'm here because I'm going along with your stupid fucking project. I'm here because I forgot to call the groom last night and tell him I wasn't coming."

"Quinn," Ellis says. "Why are you so angry?"

“Go away.” He tightens his reins, ready to leave if Ellis won’t. Half of Savannah is probably filing this scene away to chew on later. Good thing his parents don’t give a fuck that he sucks cock, unlike practically everyone else’s, who love to discuss his cock-sucking tendencies and which cock he’s sucking at any given moment. Quinn knows how Savannah talks. He talks himself. It’s the only way to live in this town.

“Quinn,” Ellis says gently. “You can tell me. Use words. What’s the anger covering up? What are you scared of or sad about? Come on. Let’s go for a ride together, you and I. We’ll go hunting another time.” The motherfucker actually takes Mister’s bridle and leads him away with Ghost. Mister’s too well-trained not to follow.

“Let go of my fucking horse!”

“Tell me what’s really wrong, and I will.”

“I don’t know!” Quinn bursts. “Do you think I know?”

“Yes,” Ellis says. “I think you do.” He pushes Ghost into a trot. Mister willingly follows, goddamn him.

“I told you. I’m never good enough.”

“Good enough for what?” Ellis asks.

His voice is so kind, so gentle, that Quinn explodes. “I wasn’t good enough for my parents and I’m never good enough for the guys I bring home and I’m not good enough for you. I’m never good enough for anyone. I’m sick of it. Might as well just — I don’t fucking know. Give up. Will you let my fucking horse go now, please?”

Quinn sees something flicker across Ellis’s face. It looks like sadness, but he isn’t sure. “I pushed you too far.”

“I shouldn’t have talked to you.” Quinn turns away from him. They’re riding through a quiet part of the woods now, down an avenue of live oaks; it probably used to be part of a plantation. Now just old and gone, past its time. Humus covers what was probably a graveled drive.

“I should have asked you to ditch the coke, start getting up in the morning, and left it. We could work on the other stuff together. I pushed too much. I didn’t know how much you hurt.

I'm so sorry. I thought you were a spoiled rich boy. I was wrong, Quinn, and I'm so sorry."

"I'm not hurt!" Quinn yells. This is probably counterproductive, but he can't stop himself. The easiest way to prove you're hurting: scream at someone that you aren't.

Ellis just looks at him sadly. "Come home with me after this," he says.

"I can't," Quinn says shortly. "Class starts today and you're the one who says I have to go, remember? Or did you fucking forget that part of the Quinn Rutledge improvement program?"

"What time does class end?" Ellis asks.

"Wouldn't you like to know." Quinn sounds eight, even to himself. He doesn't care.

"Quinn. What time do your classes end? Come over to my place, after."

"I lied. It's Friday. I don't fucking have class until Monday."

"Then just come over. Let me rub your back again."

Really fucking tempting. That back rub had been the best thing that's happened to him in months: gentle hands on him, working his muscles, not asking anything in return. "You're not going to treat me like a fucking broken toy?" he asks warily. He notices he's throwing the word 'fuck' around and Ellis hasn't commented.

"No, Quinn," Ellis says wearily. "I'm not. And I'm deeply, deeply sorry I ever made you feel that way."

"Fine," he snaps. "But only because I want a fucking back rub."

"That's fair," Ellis says.

They trot their horses back to the trailers. Quinn follows Ellis to his house. Upstairs, Quinn strips to his breeches. "You wanna take those off?" Ellis asks.

"I'm not wearing anything under them," Quinn says. He tosses a strand of blond hair out of his face.

Ellis nods. "Okay," he says. He straddles Quinn again and works on his back the way he did the night before. But this time, when he finishes, he leans over and kisses Quinn on the neck. Quinn can feel the press of Ellis's hard cock against his back. It makes him squirm with pleasure. "Do you want to play?" Ellis asks quietly. "Or would that be too much? We can just kiss, if you want."

"What kind of playing?" Quinn asks. He gets harder.

"Do you remember what I told you I wanted? You want someone to fuck you silly, by which I mean, tell you exactly what to do and how to do it, and then tuck you in and hold you until you go to sleep. If you need to, we can skip right to the tucking in and sleeping part."

Quinn feels so tempted. He wants so much to say the tucking in and sleeping part. But his cock's so stiff. He probably can't fall asleep this way.

"Take your breeches off," Ellis says, and he sounds amused. "You can borrow some boxers. I don't think they'll *quite* fall off your hips." Quinn changes with his back turned, but when he lays down his cock tents them out. Ellis pulls the light down comforter up, the sheets with an even higher thread count than Quinn's. He spoons Quinn, but brushes against him accidentally. Quinn jumps. "No wonder you turned your back," Ellis says. "Here I thought you were shy." His hand closes over Quinn. "Do you want me to, before you go to sleep?" he asks.

Quinn nods. He doesn't trust himself to talk: he's said more than he has in so long. Quinn never says anything real and the effort has taken so much out of him.

Ellis takes a moment, then wraps one arm under Quinn's neck and holds his chest. He pushes Quinn's long hair out of the way and rests his lips against his neck. "I think I remember how you did it," Ellis says. "But you tell me if I don't get it right, okay?"

Ellis slips off Quinn's boxers. And oh, he finds that perfect spot under Quinn's head and rubs at it for a long time. Then he takes Quinn's cock in his slicked hand and strokes it, not too much pressure, slow, the way Quinn likes. Ellis plays with that spot again, over and over until Quinn starts to buck a little, then jerks him harder, with more pressure, faster. It feels so good, almost exactly the way Quinn does it himself, and he goes fast, fast into Ellis's hand, shoots all over him, all over the bed. Ellis holds him and milks all of it out.

"Good?" he asks.

"Thank you," Quinn says awkwardly. He's never said thank you for this before, but it seems right.

"You don't have to say that. I wanted to. Go to sleep now. You upset yourself too much. You need to rest and everything will look better when you wake up." He kisses Quinn on the neck.

"What are you going to do?" Quinn asks.

"Sleep with you. Can I keep holding you like this?"

"Mmm-hmm. It feels good." And it does, in a comforting way, not sexual. Safe. Quinn's never slept next to anyone before. He finds that he wants to turn around and burrow into Ellis, into the good, masculine smell of him. Something like clean laundry and leather; horses.

"You're safe here," Ellis says, as if he's reading Quinn's thoughts. "You're safe. You're good enough. You're always good enough. Nothing bad happens here. Okay?"

"Okay." Quinn says. He's nearly dropped off now. Ellis kisses his neck again. It feels so good, that small kiss.

He wakes to Ellis standing over him. "Wake up, brat," he says, but he's smiling. "Lunch. Or you'll starve to death, your metabolism's so goddamn high."

"Hmm?" Quinn asks, confused. No one makes him lunch. Maybe the cook.

"Put those boxers back on and come downstairs. Pajama pants in the second drawer down so you don't flash me at the kitchen table."

Quinn obeys Ellis and stumbles downstairs. The kitchen looks huge, all battered walnut table and big windows. A sandwich waits for him, cut into neat squares, the way you slice it for a child. The big table and slanting sunlight conspire to make Quinn feel small, but not in a bad way — in a safe way, a way he never felt then. "I don't think I've had a PB&J since I was ten," he informs Ellis.

"Oh, that's not lunch. That's to keep you from starving until we go to your house, get you decent clothes, and head out to lunch, honey."

"Why are you being so nice to me all of a sudden?" Quinn asks suspiciously. "I went from not good enough to a back rub, a handjob, and a sandwich."

Ellis laughs and kisses Quinn on the head. "Because you need someone to be nice to you, Quinn," he says gently. "You haven't had anyone be nice to you in a long time, have you? You've got your friends and that's about it. But no one to take care of you. And if you're sweet today and try hard to not to say 'fuck' constantly, maybe we can play tonight."

"Play what?" Quinn asks, half-curious, half-sexy.

"Behave," Ellis warns, settling in the chair across from Quinn. He pushes a glass of milk across the table at him. "Or first thing we'll play will involve you getting punished for acting like a slutty little brat."

He looks up at Ellis and blinks sweetly. Quinn knows this game. "But I am a slutty little brat, Ellis. That's why you like me. That and you want my lips wrapped around your cock."

Ellis rolls his eyes. "That's not the reason I like you, Quinn. Eat your sandwich and stop trying to give me a hard-on. And *don't* try to touch me and *don't* play some kind of game where you get down on your knees in front of me or something. So help me god you'll get nothing if you do."

Quinn rolls *his* eyes, now. Because he was thinking about it. Bastard. He knows all the tricks before Quinn pulls them out.

"Eat your sandwich, Quinn," Ellis says gently. "Stop thinking about sex so much. I know you're nineteen, but Christ. You just got off two hours ago. Do you need to go jerk off after you finish so you can engage in civilized discourse?"

"No," Quinn says sulkily.

Ellis follows Quinn to his apartment, which suitably impresses him. He probably thought Quinn lived like some messy little frat boy. But he nods approvingly when Quinn lets him in. "You have good taste," Ellis says.

"I like to think so," Quinn says smugly.

"The proper response is 'thank you, Ellis.'"

"Thank you, Ellis," he mimics. "Do you want a drink?"

"Good manners. But no, thank you." Ellis sits on his plush velvet sectional — sits, not sprawls. Quinn loves that furniture like a baby.

"Are you actually from Savannah? You just turned down an opportunity for day-drinking." Quinn's walking up his steps, peeling his polo shirt off as he goes. He feels Ellis's eyes on him. "I might as well ask what you want me to wear, because otherwise you're going to tell me to fucking change."

"You promised to try not to say 'fuck' today," Ellis reminds him. Quinn curses under his breath. Ellis also stands and follows him up the stairs. Quinn sits on his own goddamn bed and points. "Closet. Drawers. Pick." He wishes he had thought to make his bed this morning. It's all tangled white sheets and green velvet comforter.

Shockingly, Ellis dresses him in a button down and khaki shorts, but selects a suit from his closet and zips it into a garment bag, picks out a tie, an undershirt, and some briefs. "You'll need this for dinner and you might as well keep it at my place," he says.

Quinn sighs heavily.

"Don't behave like a brat," Ellis tells him. "Act like a man, not an annoyed little boy. What's so wrong with wearing a suit?"

"I don't get why I can't wear this to dinner."

"Humor me. You look good in a well-cut suit, I like to look at you in a well-cut suit, and when you're dressed in a suit, I don't look like a lecherous old man."

"You don't look like a lecherous old man," Quinn protests. He pulls on some black briefs. Ellis watches.

"God, you look good," he comments. "Do you know how much self-control I have?"

"No," Quinn says. Brattily, he'll admit. "But I know you like me in briefs. You like the way my cock looks, don't you? You like it hard in briefs?" He drops his eyes and thinks about Ellis fucking him while he begs for it. Quinn hardens immediately.

"Goddamn you," Ellis swears. But he doesn't stop looking,

Quinn notices. That only makes him harder.

"Bet it would feel good if I played with it," he comments, almost casually. His hand wanders downward. "It'd feel better if you did it, though."

"You are *not* allowed to touch your cock," Ellis says sharply, in a deep voice. *That* voice. The voice Quinn can never resist obeying. He's heard it once or twice before and it never fails to elicit complete and total obedience from him, even as it makes him rock-hard. He drops his hands to his sides and lowers his eyes.

"I'm sorry, Ellis," he says.

"Put your clothes on like a civilized human," Ellis says in that same deep voice. "Then maybe, if you can behave, I'll take you to lunch and I *won't* punish you tonight for being a bratty little slut and teasing me."

"Yessir." It slips out, but it feels right.

"Good."

Quinn dresses in silence, eyes downcast. He also makes his bed. He feels, somehow, like he ought to. Luckily he keeps his room fairly picked up.

They go back to Ellis's car. Quinn doesn't talk, but Ellis holds his hand. Quinn feels chastised, like he should have known better, but that Ellis has forgiven him and is making an effort to ensure that he knows it. Ellis opens the car door for Quinn, who almost complains that he's not a goddamn girl, but stops himself. Instead he slides into the leather seat and buckles his seatbelt like he knows Ellis wants him to.

"Next question," Ellis says, as he drives up Drayton. "With all your extracurricular activities... when were you last tested?"

"Last month and I'm clean!" Quinn snaps. God. Like he'd take risks with something that important. Quinn will admit he's sort of a slut. But he's not an irresponsible slut.

"Always use condoms?"

"Yes!" Jesus. What kind of dumbass doesn't use condoms?

"Never suck dick?"

"Um, yeah?" What does Ellis think he does with these guys? Play fucking Parcheesi?

"You let them finish in your mouth?"

"No," Quinn says. "God." Not like St. Albert's had a comprehensive sex ed program — it mostly amounted to "don't do it, and if you do, here's some horrifying slides of STD-ridden genitals, plus a horrifyingly graphic video of childbirth", which had made both him and Isabel Sims faint — but Quinn has Google.

"You need tested anyway. After lunch, we're going to the clinic." Ellis steers calmly through the Savannah traffic. Quinn folds his arms and slumps back on the seat. *God.* Like he'd take risks like that. Does Ellis think he acts like some kind of idiot? Yeah, Quinn might fuck around with a lot of guys, but he knows what safe sex means.

"You can still get certain STDs just from giving head, even if they don't come in your mouth, you know," Ellis says. Quinn stares out the window and makes a noise. He didn't know that but he won't give Ellis the satisfaction of admitting it.

"Didn't you see that episode of *Degrassi Junior High*?" Ellis presses. "Where Emma gets throat gonorrhea from blowing Jay in a van down by the river?"

"Aren't you a little old to watch *Degrassi Junior High*?" Quinn snarks, just to get back at Ellis. But he totally remembers watching that episode one day at Henry's when they had nothing better to do. "And it was in the ravine."

"I got bored one day and there was nothing better on TV." Ellis shrugs. "And no playing until your results come back."

Quinn sighs heavily. "Why don't you take me home after lunch then?"

"Why don't you come back to my house, get another back rub, go to dinner in a suit like a civilized person, and then you can make a decision about whether or not you'd like to spend the night? And Sunday you can sleep in, no one hunts on Sunday. But I'll expect you for brunch at nine."

"Seriously?" Quinn demands. "I don't get to sleep in *at all*?"

"In a suit."

"Jesus fuck."

"Quinn," Ellis says. He uses what Quinn has grown to recognize as his warning voice.

"Sorry," he tells the older man. "I'm trying. I swear I'm trying." He throws Ellis his best pleading face. Ellis glances at him. Those green eyes and that long hair. Quinn wants to tangle his hands in it while Ellis fucks him.

"I know how hard it can be," Ellis tells him. "*Believe* me." He stops, gets out, and tosses his keys to the valet at Chester B. Arthur. The valet opens the door for Quinn. Ellis takes his hand and leads him inside. No one ever holds Quinn's hand. In fact, he can't *remember* the last time someone other than Ellis held his hand. Maybe never: relatives and nannies don't count. The maitre'd leads them to a posh back table. Ellis always seems to score the good tables. "What do you want?" he asks Quinn abruptly.

Quinn rattles off a salad, an appetizer, and a main course. "Still growing?" Ellis asks.

Quinn smirks.

Ellis rolls his eyes. But he orders everything Quinn asks for. And doesn't drop Quinn's hand. Instead, he sets it on top of the table and plays with it. This is *definitely* the first time anyone's done this with Quinn. "So what do you do in equine studies?" Ellis asks.

Quinn reels off a long list of his coursework, including the work actually done on horseback.

"So how many horses do you have?" Ellis asks.

"Three right now," Quinn replies. "Zelda for dressage, Lucifer for eventing, and Mister for hunting. I keep the other two at the SASA stables." He shifts on the overstuffed seats. Quinn can't stop thinking about the damn clinic. He fucking hates needles, mostly because he has a tendency to pass out when he gets stuck, but no way will he share that with Ellis. No. Fucking. Way. Too embarrassing. And part of Quinn wants to be a dick. Ellis wants him to get tested? Let him see Quinn hit the table.

True to his word, after lunch, Ellis drives him to the clinic near the edge of downtown. "All confidential," the nurse assures Quinn as he fills out the paperwork. "No insurance. No records.

We should have your results in 24 hours." Ellis pays. Quinn thinks about arguing and decides not to. Fuck it. Ellis wants Quinn tested, Ellis can pay for it. Fair's fair.

They take Quinn back. "Do you want your boyfriend to come back with you?"

Quinn's mouth twists. "Sure," he says. He still sort of wants Ellis to see *exactly* what's going to happen. Part of him just wants to be mean. Part of him's genuinely curious. First the nurse makes him pee in a cup, standard, then points him to an exam table. Quinn carefully sits on the far end so that when he goes straight back, he'll only hit the bed. The shaking sets in.

"You okay?" Ellis asks, brows knitted. He rubs Quinn's back.

"Yeah," Quinn says, as best as he can muster. No, he is definitely not okay. He hopes Ellis will notice. He really wants Ellis to notice. But Ellis doesn't seem to. His funeral. He wants Quinn to get stuck? He can damn well see what happens. Quinn makes sure to watch the needle go in. As soon as it pierces his skin, everything tunnels to black.

He wakes flat on his back, blinky, confused. Where is he? Oh yeah, the clinic. Ellis hovers over him. "You didn't tell me you passed out!"

"I don't always?" Quinn says. His voice sounds weak and tired, even to him.

"Christ," Ellis says.

The paper under him crinkles. Quinn tries to sit and everything spins. "No, stay down," Ellis says wearily. "You're going to pass out again if you don't. Give it time. You knew this would happen, didn't you?"

"No?"

"Yes you fucking did. Because if it happens, it usually happens every goddamn time. And you just ate so don't try to tell me your blood sugar was low." Ellis helps Quinn sit. The nurse tries to hand him juice, but Ellis intervenes.

"No, you know you'll spill it, Quinn. God. Don't make this worse." He holds it and gives Quinn little sips. The nurse glares at Ellis.

"Poor thing," she coos.

"Poor thing nothing, he's trying to get back at me for dragging him here in the first place," Ellis tells her. "Which is why he didn't see fit to inform us that needles make him faint."

The nurse throws Quinn some serious side-eye. "You're fine to go," she says. "Don't fall on your way out."

Ellis helps Quinn into the car. "Do you know how much you scared me? If you had those test results in your hand I would —"

"You'd what?" Quinn asks, but it doesn't come out as smirky as he'd like, because he's so tired. "Tell me *exactly* what kind of punishment I'd get, Ellis."

Ellis glares. "I wouldn't. You'd like it too much. I'd just take your ass home. Which is what I'm doing. Show up tomorrow with your test in hand, say you're sorry, and we can talk."

True to his word, Ellis drops Quinn back to his own apartment. "See you tomorrow."

"Or not," Quinn snaps.

Ellis snorts. "Uh-huh. I'll see you after lunch, sweetheart. Behave yourself tonight. If I find out you went out clubbing, I *will not* be happy. Call Delia, hang out with her and her spacey little bestie — Isabel? Go see some of your other friends — the Jasper twins? That Hendricks boy, the carpenter? He redid my house."

"How do you know who my fucking friends are?!" Quinn demands.

Ellis shrugs. "Savannah likes liquor and gossip, in that order."

Quinn slams his metal door, which crashes satisfyingly. He plays some video games and eventually calls Crispin Hendricks. Crispin's bored and miserable — he just moved back from Athens after a summer with his boyfriend, Henry's twin Wills. "Wanna call Lucky and Thor and get drunk?" Crispin asks.

"Fuck yeah," Quinn says.

They all end up at Frog and Toad, which never cards, taking shots. Quinn beats everyone but Lucky. Maybe Thor, not like you can tell them apart, matching loose brown curls and brown eyes, and maybe Lucky made Thor switch just to fuck with everyone. Crispin sucks down liquor because he misses Wills. "I gave him a ring," he says sadly. "Like not a ring-ring. But a promise. I miss him so fucking much." He orders another shot. "You seeing anyone?"

Quinn tells him about the weirdness that's Ellis. "And he won't fuck me!" he bitches.

"Probably good for you," Crispin says. He shakes his corkscrewed blond curls and downs the shot of whiskey.

"It's weird," Quinn says. He sips at his scotch and soda.

"You like it," Lucky tells him. Quinn knows it's Lucky because Thor wouldn't say that.

Quinn reddens. "Shut up," he snaps. And orders another shot.

CHAPTER 4

Quinn knew he'd pass out. He resented going to the clinic and he resented Ellis saying they could fool around, then taking it back. Seeing Quinn's eyes roll back and him falling backwards — Ellis's stomach had dropped; his pulse had shot up; he'd drawn a breath to scream for a doctor: he knew what an OD looked like, thanks to Logan. Then Ellis realized the needle had made Quinn faint. And Quinn had known the needle would make him faint. And Quinn had declined to share that information, just to see what Ellis would do. So Ellis takes his drama queen ass home and tells him to come back when he has test results and says he's sorry. Which sucks. But Quinn has to learn he can't pull shit like this. He can't scare the hell out of Ellis just to get a reaction.

Ellis prays Quinn will show up the next day. He feels fairly sure Quinn will come. But you never know, with the kind of hurt Quinn's been through. You just never fucking know. He tries reading, but Fitzgerald's short stories swim on the page. He tries cooking, uses up all the flour, makes a pasta salad, and can't figure out what else to do. So he resorts to cleaning, even though he pays a maid for that. He's changing the sheets when he hears a knock at the door, sometime around three.

Ellis lets out a breath he didn't know he was holding. He opens the door to Quinn standing on the front steps, all dressed up like a frat boy. "I brought a suit before you bitch," he says. "And

I'm clean." He hands a piece of paper to Ellis. "Here's the proof. Happy now?"

Ellis kisses him on the forehead. "Good," he murmurs. "What a good boy." It slips out before he can stop himself, and he curses inwardly. "Have you had lunch?"

"No," Quinn says.

Not a shock. Of course he hasn't eaten. Quinn doesn't take care of himself.

Ellis leads him to the kitchen, and points at a chair. "Sit," he orders. He turns on the stove and begins cracking eggs into a pan.

"What are you doing?" Quinn asks.

"Feeding you an omelet. You're still growing. At least I suspect you are, based on your consumption of food in general. How the hell have you managed not to eat today?"

Quinn shrugs. "I wasn't around anything."

Ellis doesn't mention that he was probably at his apartment all day. That tells him all he needs to know about the food Quinn keeps in his fridge: probably nothing but condiments. "You have to take care of yourself."

Ellis glances back from the stove. Quinn shrugs again. "I do."

"You don't. And you didn't eat because you're hungover," he says, taking in Quinn's red-rimmed eyes, the bags under them. "Which bar?"

"Huh?"

"Which bar did you and your friends get drunk at?"

"Frog and Toad doesn't card." Quinn rubs his temples. Ellis sighs. After he sets the omelet in front of Quinn, he fetches him some aspirin and mixes up an Alka-Seltzer. "Drink it all," he says. "One true cure for a hangover."

Quinn looks up slightly belligerently. "How d'you know?"

"That's what my father used to say. You think I've never seen someone hungover?"

Obediently, Quinn scarfs the food — of course, he was half-starved — then drinks the Alka-Seltzer in one long chug. Probably dehydrated. Ellis brings him a Gatorade, one he keeps for when he's working out. He hands it wordlessly to Quinn, who downs it.

"Better?" Ellis asks.

Quinn nods. "Thank you," he says, without meeting Ellis's eyes. Ellis senses he's embarrassed. No one's ever really fussed over Quinn before, it seems, and he doesn't quite know how to deal with the attention, as much as Ellis can see he craves it. So much *why me?* in his whole attitude. Quinn flew into a rage the other night because he doesn't think he's good enough and he loathes when people remind him of it.

"Quinn?" Ellis says gently, once he's finished the Gatorade and looks down at the table, seemingly unsure of what to do next. "You want to stay down here and watch TV, or you want to go upstairs?"

"What's upstairs mean?" Quinn asks. He seems skittish, this brat who tried to tease Ellis yesterday by stroking his own cock through those goddamn briefs. Ellis thinks about it; thinks hard. Quinn wants the attention, the omelets, the Gatorade. He craves someone to take care of him. But Quinn associates sex with people leaving. If he sleeps with Ellis, Ellis will leave. Probably subconscious, but it's there.

"Quinn, we only go upstairs if you want to. And if we do I won't leave afterwards or kick you out or decide not to see you again," Ellis says. "We can always stay down here and watch a movie, if you'd rather."

"No," Quinn says. "I asked what it *meant.*"

Ellis shrugs. "What do you want it to mean?"

Quinn bites his lip. He looks down again and looks back up without raising his chin. Ellis hardens almost immediately — god, Quinn knows how to destroy him. "No," he says. "What do *you* want it to mean? Sir?" And this "sir" doesn't have that snarky little twist to it.

Ellis takes a deep breath. He needs to control himself. "Quinn, you're killing me."

"What do you mean?" he asks, with the same posture, with those big eyes, blue today, blinking innocently. It doesn't help that Quinn's sitting and Ellis's standing. "Do you want me to do something, Ellis?"

Ellis's carefully maintained self-control snaps, a breaking thing stretched too far. "Get upstairs," he says, using his deep, commanding voice. "Now." Quinn stands, politely pushes in his chair, and walks up to Ellis's bedroom. He goes inside, kneels on the floor, clasps his hands behind his back, head lowered, and waits. Sweet Jesus. Ellis's harder just walking in the goddamn door. It doesn't help that Quinn's tenting his shorts. Perfectly innocent, ready to do whatever Ellis asks. God, he's clearly played sub before and it's delicious.

God, what a picture: Quinn's blond head bowed down, his hair a curtain over his face, his hard cock jutting out. Ellis wants to grab that hair and fuck his mouth, make Quinn take it just because he looks so pretty kneeling there. But he has to be gentle. Quinn needs it. More than that, Quinn *deserves* it. He expects Ellis to walk into the room, fuck his mouth, and kick him out. Ellis has to make this different for him. Quinn needs taken care of. "Quinn," Ellis says, so goddamn reluctantly. "Get off your knees."

"What did I do?" He sounds panicked. "Isn't this how you want me?"

"Not right now. Eventually. But not now. Now it just plays into every fucking insecurity you have. Get up."

"Not supposed to say 'fuck,'" Quinn smirks.

"Shut up and get in bed," Ellis orders. "Brat. Take off your shirt and shorts first. You don't get in bed with your clothes on. Just your briefs."

"You like my briefs," Quinn says. "You like me in briefs *a lot*, Ellis."

"I do," Ellis says. "They make your cock look good. Get in bed." If he acknowledges it, he hopes Quinn will stop teasing him about it. And wear them all the goddamn time for him.

Ellis strips to his boxers. He watches Quinn as he lies on his back. Hard, of course. His hand slides below his washboard stomach and he begins rubbing himself. He makes a small noise, holds himself, and plays on that sweet spot under his head. Ellis loftily ignores him.

"You like watching, Ellis," Quinn taunts.

"And you like being watched." Ellis lies next to him and pulls the covers over them: the white sheets, the light down comforter. It seems to startle Quinn. "Come here."

Quinn immediately presses against Ellis, his lean, muscled chest against Ellis's, that delicious hard cock tucked in those briefs deliberately rubbing against his own. Quinn tangles his legs up with Ellis's. "What?" he asks.

"I should spank the hell out of you," Ellis says. He tugs Quinn's hair. God, he's wanted to do that sofuckingbad. Quinn's hair was made for pulling. "I asked you to come here, not burrow into me."

"But you feel so good," Quinn says, big eyes looking up at him, mischief flickering in them. "Daddy."

Ellis immediately hardens further. His breath catches. That fucking brat. Of course Quinn notices. His lip pouts out. "Daddy?" Quinn says, his voice rising into a question. Big blue eyes, Ellis's hands tangled in that hair. Ellis should spank Quinn's ass red for acting like such a little slut. And he would, if he weren't so goddamn hard. Dammit, Ellis tries *so fucking much* to shove this down. He isn't supposed to think like this. It's not ... it's not the type of thing you can talk about. It's not acceptable. It's not *normal.*

"What, Quinn?" he asks, his voice careful, even. Ellis has learned that much self-control, at least.

"Are you gonna fuck me now?" Quinn asks. "I really want you to fuck me now. I'll be such a good boy for you." He picks up Ellis's hand. "See how hard you made my cock, Daddy?"

Ellis's dying over that sweet little voice. Quinn has him now and he knows it. He's going to get whatever he wants out of Ellis, godfuckingdammit. Ellis has waited too long to play this game, and his self-control is close to snapping again.

"No," Ellis says. "I'm not going to fuck you, Quinn. You're being a brat."

"How am I being a brat?" Quinn asks. "I'm doing everything you're asking, Daddy." His lower lip trembles a little. That tiny little quiver, *oh god.*

Suddenly Ellis realizes: Oh *fuck,* this isn't just his kink.

This is Quinn's kink.

This is *more than* Quinn's kink.

I'm not good enough. I'm never good enough.

Quinn fucking his way through the gay population of greater Savannah. Quinn getting ignored by his parents. Quinn coming back to get bossed around. Quinn eating up any little kindnesses Ellis doles out. Quinn wanting to hold his hand. Quinn passing out at the clinic, trying to get back at Ellis, yes, but also, in a fucked up way, trying to make Ellis comfort him when he was hurt. Quinn turning up hungry and hungover—

Quinn's not just teasing him. Quinn's feeling him out. Quinn isn't merely tormenting him, calling him Daddy. Quinn wants to know if Ellis will *let him* call him Daddy. And if Ellis will agree to play the role. Which, as much as Ellis tries to push it to the back of his mind, to shove it away, he desperately wants to do. Ellis has waited for this, has craved it, no matter how much he's sublimated it and ignored it and shunted it onto some other impulse. Ellis wants a boy so badly; a boy to cuddle and care for and love and fuck.

They've held each other at arm's length. He calls Quinn "brat." Quinn sneeringly calls him "sir" or just plain Ellis.

All at once, Ellis lets it go. He wants this and he thinks Quinn wants this and why the fuck not? The desire almost chokes him. "You are doing everything I ask, sweet boy," Ellis manages. "You're being so good."

Quinn lights up. His eyes widen; he squirms a little in Ellis's arms. "Am I? Am I being good? I'm trying so hard, Daddy."

Ellis kisses his forehead. "I know you're trying, sweet boy." He's so fucking hard right now. He rubs against Quinn. Quinn eagerly thrusts back. "You need fucked, don't you?"

"Mmm-hmm. Please, Daddy?" Quinn grinds against him shamelessly and cuddles closer. "I'll do anything you ask. I'll be so, so good you won't believe it. Please?"

"Here, turn over on your side, boy," Ellis says. Quinn will like this, and at his age, with his experience, he's probably never done it. Ellis grabs the lube from the side table. "Be a good boy and take everything off for me."

Obediently, Quinn removes his underwear. "Now, don't touch your cock," Ellis says sternly, but indulgently, kindly. "I know you'll want to but I'll tell you when. So be a good boy and keep your hands off it. It's mine, and you're not allowed to play with it unless Daddy says so. Do you understand?"

"Yes, Daddy," Quinn says. Oh god. Ellis has wanted to hear those words forever.

Ellis gently bends Quinn's leg at the knee and guides it upwards to spread him, then strokes lube onto Quinn's ass, oh, that perfect little pucker he's been jerking off about. Quinn purrs. "That feels so good," he says. "Are you going to pet my ass now? Will you do it the way I like?"

"I'll have to figure out what you like, sweet boy," Ellis says. He strokes, then circles. Quinn still whines a little, and keeps whining until Ellis starts fucking two fingers in and out a little bit, at first not even past his tight ring. Then he hums with pleasure and arches his back. "Like that, baby boy?" he asks. "You like when I fuck my fingers in your ass?"

"Mmm-hmm."

"Tell Daddy how much you like it. I like to hear my boy talk."

"I like it so much, Daddy," Quinn says. "Do it deeper and deeper."

Ellis uses a lot of lube and slowly, carefully, opens Quinn up, fucking him a little deeper every time and oh god, Quinn feels so tight, and knowing he gets to fuck that tight little ass while Quinn calls him Daddy has Ellis almost painfully stiff. He finally crooks his fingers and presses, finding that spot he knows Quinn will like, and Quinn cries out, wiggling wantonly on him." Good boy," Ellis says. "What a good little slut for Daddy. You want more?"

"Please Daddy please I'm not full enough yet. Please?" Quinn's growing breathless. Carefully, Ellis works another finger into his tight muscles. He slowly strokes them, relaxes them. "Breathe for Daddy," he says. "C'mon, Q baby. You can do it. Relax, baby boy. That's it. This'll feel so good."

His third finger gradually joins the others. He fucks Quinn with them, who soon starts bucking and whimpering and begging. "Can I have your cock, Daddy? Can I please have your cock? Will you fuck me now, Daddy?"

"Have you been a good boy, Quinn?" he asks, a little sternly.

"I've tried," Quinn says. "I promise I try so hard." He arches on Ellis's fingers.

"I'll go slow, okay, sweet boy? But I can't see your face so you have to tell me if it hurts. Will you tell me if it hurts?"

"Yes, Daddy."

Ellis doesn't bother with a condom; Quinn's clean and so is he. His boxers come off; he slicks himself, then nudges at Quinn's now-slicked entrance. "Open up for me," he says. "C'mon now, sweet boy." As he begins to push inside, he feels that luxurious stretching, that wonderful opening as Quinn's tight circle widens for him. "Good boy," Ellis says, working him a little. "What a sweet boy, to let me in like this. Such a good boy with such a tight ass."

Quinn groans.

Ellis slowly slides into him. Quinn's ring stays so tight. When Ellis's head touches that good spot, Quinn shudders and makes a small sound. "Oh, good boy," Ellis tells him, settling into him, pressing against his back. "You're so tight and hot for Daddy. What a good boy."

He lies still. Quinn moans on him and moves slightly so Ellis's cock rubs his prostate. Ellis rests his lips on Quinn's neck and rocks in him. He's so tight and hot, oh god, whimpering and twisting on him. Ellis feels his muscles tautening. He holds Quinn tight and strokes over his body.

"Are you close, baby boy?" Ellis asks.

"I'm so close, Daddy," Quinn moans.

"What'll make you go and what'll make you last?"

"I think I'm going to go unless you stay totally still, Daddy, I'm so full. Your cock's so big, Daddy and it feels so good, and when you talk to me I get so hard. If you fuck me and talk to me at the same time I'll come so much."

"I want to feel it, sweet boy." Ellis begins moving in and out of him. "Come for me, baby. Let me feel you shoot hot come for me. C'mon, baby boy. Show Daddy how much you come at once."

Quinn almost immediately arches against him and loses it. Ellis keeps fucking him, breathlessly, hard. "That's it," he whispers into his ear. "Come hard for me. Wanna see you come a lot, baby. I like all that sticky come from my sweet boy." Quinn makes all sorts of nonsense noises, bucks and shoots and keeps going. Ellis can't take it anymore and goes along with him, a hot flood in Quinn's tight ass that sends Quinn moaning again, *that's so good Daddy, oh god Daddy, come in my ass, I love your hot come in my ass*. He only pushes Ellis's climax to last longer, to feel more intense.

They finally both finish. Ellis holds Quinn and doesn't move for a long time. When he finally slips out, he brushes Quinn's cheek. Quinn turns, sleepy-eyed. Ellis finds his lips and kisses him gently, plays, sucks and tastes. He draws the languid, lazy kiss out for a long time. You don't kiss guys you just bring home to fuck. He knows it and Quinn knows it.

"You were a good boy, Quinn," Ellis says. He strokes down the length of Quinn's side.

"I tried to be, Daddy," Quinn tells him shyly. He buries his head in Ellis's chest and wraps around him. Oh god, his thighs are sticky. Oh *fuck* that's hot. Ellis wants him again now.

"You liked that," Ellis says. "You want a daddy, don't you? Tell me the truth, Quinn."

Quinn doesn't answer. He only nestles closer into Ellis, a warm, lithe little bundle all tangled up with him. They've kicked off the blankets. Ellis pulls them back on. Quinn's smaller than he is, and Ellis doesn't want him to get cold.

"Quinn," Ellis says gently after a few moments. "Tell me what you want." It's easier to say, even without sex, knowing Quinn wants it too. "Do you want a daddy?"

"Yeah," Quinn finally says quietly. "Yeah, I guess I do." He sounds like he's admitting something that frightens him in its enormity.

"What do you think that means?" Ellis asks. He keeps his voice low and soft, and he strokes Quinn's hair.

Quinn shrugs. Ellis has noticed that Quinn talks a lot, but he doesn't often say very much. He realizes, with a start, Quinn doesn't think he has very much to say at all.

"C'mon, sweet boy," Ellis coaxes. "You tell me what it means to you, and I'll tell you what it means to me, okay?"

"Like you said the other night," Quinn stumbles. "Someone to take care of me and pet me and cuddle me and fuck me too, but — I don't know. Like you said." He burrows closer to Ellis, and Ellis realizes he's the first person to listen to Quinn in a very long time.

"I want to take care of you," Ellis says gently. He pets Quinn's blond head. "I want to help you Quinn. You're kind of a mess, baby. And I know you're unhappy."

Quinn curls up a little tighter.

"I know you're lonely."

Quinn curls up tighter still.

"Sweet boy, you can tell me," Ellis says. He can almost feel the sadness coming off Quinn in waves. If you can touch a person and feel them lost, Quinn is lost, and has been for a very long time.

"You're shit at pillow talk, Ellis," Quinn replies. His voice shakes a little.

"Quinn," Ellis says, and lets a little bit of warning sneak into his voice. "Tell me how you feel. You don't have to hide it from me. I want to help you get better, baby boy."

"'M sad. And lonely." He talks to Ellis's chest, not to his face. "I've always been sad and lonely, since I can remember. No one wants me around. So I just don't. Stay around, I mean. It's easier."

"I want you around, honey. I'd be happy to have you in my bed every single night, to cuddle you to sleep, to take care of you, and to make sure you were a good boy. Would you be a good boy for me, Quinn?" Those long, sticky thighs are distracting. He wants to finger Quinn and feel how slick his ass is.

"Yes," Quinn says eagerly. "I'd be so good, Daddy."

"That means you'd *go to class.* No drugs. No crazy partying. Waking up early and civilizing yourself. If you're bad, you get punished. Do you understand that?"

"What's punished mean?" Quinn asks suspiciously.

"You'll get spanked. I won't let you get off. Extra chores, but you do them naked. All sorts of things. You'd also get to play all kinds of fun games. But only if you want to."

Quinn perks up. "What kind of games, Daddy?"

"I'll teach you all kinds of things. You were so good to come in here and get down on your knees for me. What a good boy. Do you know how hard it was not to fuck your pretty mouth, with that hard cock and all that blond hair? I'll teach you how to wear a cock ring so you last longer, and you'll get all kinds of fun toys to play with. I'd play with you until you were so tired you couldn't play anymore. Would you like that?"

"Maybe," Quinn says shyly.

"I'll teach you how to be a good boy and be patient and wait for what you want. Do you think you could learn that? I'd play with you as much as you'd let me, sweet boy."

"I'd like that," Quinn says. Ellis realizes he's doing something with his hand and grabs at him suddenly. Brat's hard already and playing with his cock. It's not a little hard either; Quinn's standing stiff.

"Quinn," Ellis says, warning in his voice. "You're obsessed with sex. One of the first rules: you're not allowed to touch your cock unless I give you permission."

"Daddy!" Quinn protests. "That's not fair!"

"It is when you need to learn self-control. No touching. You can always ask permission. But I can always say no."

"Can I play with my cock?" Quinn asks sweetly.

"No, you may not. You just came all over my sheets, you're

probably still sticky, and we haven't cleaned up from last time. You may not play with your cock, Quinn."

Quinn huffs.

"The second rule is no sulking."

He earns a sigh.

"You know what the rest are. Wake up early and stay away from drugs, and go to class. Don't party. We'll work on the rest of them together, okay, sweet boy?" Ellis makes his voice gentle again.

Just that change in tone flips a switch in Quinn so immediately that Ellis feels guilty. "Okay, Daddy," he says, and cuddles into Ellis's chest again. Still stiff, of course. But at least he's ignoring it and showing some semblance of self-control. They clean up, but Ellis does it as quickly as possible — partly so he doesn't have those sticky thighs as a distraction, partly so he can nestle Quinn back into him. He feels like a small, hurt thing. God, Ellis would have done anything to have this when he was Quinn's age. Anything. He remembers the ashen taste of unwantedness, of covering it up with drugs and parties and sex. Never drinking. Drugs, but never drinking.

"You wanna go to sleep like this?" Ellis asks, playing with Quinn's hair. "You're a sleeper, baby boy, aren't you?"

"Mmm-hmm, Daddy, I think so. I just never had anyone to sleep *with* so I'm not really sure? But I think I am. I always feel so tired and heavy afterwards."

"I'm a sleeper." Ellis laughs. "I always nap after sex. Here. Put your head right here." Ellis lies on his back and pulls Quinn half onto his chest. Quinn wraps around him and yawns.

"You feel good," Quinn says. He sounds so sleepy. He and Ellis have sunk into the down mattress, the down comforter, the down pillows, the white sheets.

"Go to sleep, sweet boy. I'll wake you for dinner."

"Mmmkay, Daddy," Quinn slurs. He's already asleep.

CHAPTER 5

Quinn wakes confused.

He's tangled up with someone, cock hard; the sheets feel soft and everything's fluffy-warm. The someone holds him; his head rests on the someone's chest while an arm runs down his back and cups his ass. Quinn opens his eyes. Ellis. He's in Ellis's bed. *Daddy.*

Oh, *fuck*.

What the *fuck* came out of his mouth?

Do you want a daddy, Quinn?

Yeah, I think I do.

Oh, *fuck*.

Quinn has tried to ignore this *forever.* He has the internet. He knows what Daddy kink is. And yeah, so what if he spends a good deal of time jerking himself while he thinks about it? And not always the sex part, either. It sneaks in, it always has: *I'll be a good boy, I'll be so good for you.* But Quinn emphatically does *not* indulge himself. That would be weird. Who does that kind of thing?

Apparently Ellis.

Apparently Quinn.

Oh, *fuck*.

But it felt so *good* to call Ellis "Daddy." He loved getting fucked while Ellis called him a sweet boy, a good boy, oh god Quinn was close *before* Ellis slid that big cock into his ass. And then Ellis said he'd take care of Quinn and pet him and cuddle him and play with him as much as he wanted. Plus back rubs whenever he asked if he was being good.

Fuck it. Quinn can call Ellis whatever the fuck he wants.

And Quinn can be so good.

Just thinking about how good he can be, Quinn's wake-up hard-on becomes something else. He wants to play with it. It would feel so good to stroke himself, to rub that spot under his head and think about Ellis — Daddy —

Maybe Ellis would want to play again.

Maybe Ellis would want Quinn to suck him off.

Maybe Ellis would want to fuck him again. He *said* he would play with Quinn until he was exhausted, and Quinn, his hard cock pressing against Ellis, is decidedly *not* exhausted.

"Daddy?" Quinn says quietly. "Daddy?"

"Q?" Ellis yawns and turns to him. "I didn't think you'd wake up before me, sweet boy."

"I couldn't not wake up." Quinn figures acting helpless is his best chance.

"Why's that, honey?"

"I'm so hard, Daddy. See?" He lays Ellis's hand on his cock. "I woke up like this and I was pressed against you and I can't go back to sleep."

Ellis laughs a little. "What time is it? You just got off three hours ago, sweet boy. And feel this hard cock. Did you get this hard for me?"

"Uh-huh." Ellis begins to fondle him. Just a little bit. Quinn wants it so much. He presses against Ellis's hand.

"You need to learn self-control," Ellis says sternly.

"Can you play with me?" Quinn asks. "Please?" He pauses. "I was so good and I didn't touch it myself. I waited to ask permission." That should convince him.

"Oh, you were good, weren't you?" Ellis breathes, and Quinn *knows* he's said the right thing. "You were such a good boy to listen. Good boys get rewards for doing for what they're told. What do you want, baby?"

"I wanna play."

"How do you wanna play?"

Quinn snuggles close and buries his head in Ellis's chest. It feels so good to cede control of everything, to hand it to someone else. Quinn always controls his interactions with other men. He decides what happens, where it happens, who does what. The top just plays the role he allows. He doesn't bring home men who wouldn't. But there's a small spark, something fragile and precious, growing between them. Quinn trusts him —not completely, but enough.

Quinn hasn't had this since Calhoun.

"How do *you* wanna play?" Quinn asks, and he isn't just acting out what Ellis wants. "I wanna play how you wanna play." He feels himself get stiffer in Ellis's hand. Ellis notices.

"What a good boy you are," Ellis nearly purrs. "What a good boy you're being today. Do you want fucked again, sweet boy? Do you want me to get you close and then fuck you?"

"Uh-huh, Daddy," Quinn says. He wraps around Ellis and tilts his chin up at him, begging. "Please?"

Ellis brushes Quinn's hair out of his face. His lips feel gentle. Quinn isn't used to this. If kisses come, they come with hard, demanding need, not soft sucking, not playing. Not someone cupping his face and stroking his neck. Reflexively, he grabs the back of Ellis's neck and tries to deepen it. Daddy stops him.

"None of that, little brat," he says affectionately. "Learn to enjoy it." He returns to his patient toying, one arm slipped under Quinn's neck and down his back, the other petting his side. Quinn mimics Ellis. When he finally nips gently, Quinn gasps.

"You liked that, baby Q?" Ellis asks. He bites Quinn's neck, so carefully, and Quinn sucks in another breath. Ellis laughs quietly. "Little twink likes to get bitten," he says. But he keeps it up, nibbling and tasting him all over. He grinds slowly against Quinn's cock, but when Quinn starts bucking, Ellis firmly stills his hips. "No, you learn to go slow, little one," he says. "You want it so fast."

"But Daddy, I'm so *hard*," Quinn says. He knows he's whining.

"Then I'll hold it for you while we kiss." Ellis's hand wraps around him. But true to his word, he only grips Quinn lightly; he doesn't jerk him or stroke. Maddening. Quinn takes Ellis in hand and does the same, just to be bratty. Ellis sighs a little into Quinn's mouth. Quinn holds his big, heavy balls. He lifts them, weighs them, all the time whimpering and whining while Ellis nips at him.

"Get on your knees with your head on the pillow," Ellis says. "The angle's easiest." And oh, Quinn's going to get fingered *and* jerked. Lube touches his ass, fingers play gently over him while Daddy slicks Quinn's cock and jacks him slowly. Two fingers slip inside and begin to open him up. It's easier; Ellis fucked him not long ago, and Quinn realizes with a slight shiver of pleasure that his ass is still sticky with come. Slowly, Ellis's fingers slide deeper and deeper until they rest against Quinn's prostrate and stroke, pet, tap. Quinn squirms and makes pleased little sounds, stretching his ass toward Ellis.

"You like that, sweet boy? Tell me how much you like it when I finger your ass."

"It feels so good, Daddy. I want more. Please fuck me with them and give me more." Quinn moves on him, trying for friction, for anything.

"Shh. You're impatient. I'll break you of that." His hand slows on Quinn's cock; Quinn whines. But another finger slips at his entrance while Ellis presses outward to stretch his tight muscles. "C'mon, baby. That's it. Open up for me. C'mon," Ellis sweet-talks. Quinn loves that. Then that finger glides in, and there's that too-full feeling, that stretching burn. Quinn tenses then remembers to breathe. Ellis strokes his back. "Good boy," he says. "Hush, it'll be so good. C'mon baby." Then it *is*, and Ellis starts fucking him with his fingers, always hitting the right spot inside Quinn, and he starts to meet Ellis halfway. The nonsense starts. *Oh yeah fuck me, that's it, please fuck my tight ass, I love it when you finger my tight ass, I'm so ready for your cock, fuck me, please fuck me.*

"You're being rude," Ellis admonishes. "How do we ask?" His fingers slow.

"Please fuck me, Daddy?" Quinn asks sweetly. "Please? I'm so ready for you. You can feel how hard I am. I'll come so hard for you."

Ellis's fingers withdraw and Quinn feels him at his entrance. Ellis suddenly smacks Quinn's hole with his dick. Quinn moans. "That's for not asking nicely, brat," Ellis tells him. He smacks his ass several more times, and it's maddening, but so hot. "That's for your impatience. Now tell me you're sorry for misbehaving."

"I'm so sorry Daddy," Quinn says contritely as he can manage. "Please fuck me now, Daddy? I'll be good now, I promise. I'll be sweet and good and ask nicely for things."

Ellis's head begins opening him up. There's a familiar stretching, the burn of it as Quinn's delicate ridges spread apart. He feels too full. Ellis pets him. "Good boy," he says. "What a good boy. That's it. Good boy. Almost there."

Then he hits that spot and Quinn wiggles and whimpers with pleasure.

"Is that it, sweet boy? Did Daddy get his cock right where you wanted it?"

"Uh-huh," Quinn manages. "Please fuck me. Please please fuck me Daddy. I'll be so good. I'll be so so good."

Ellis starts moving inside him, little tiny thrusts that rub against Quinn's prostate. Quinn moans. "I bet you'll come without me touching your cock," Ellis says. "Let me see it. C'mon. You can do it. Come for me, you're so ready. Let me see all that hot, sticky come from my boy." Quinn was ready before he slid inside and their balls slapping together, combined with Ellis's stroking, push him quickly to the edge. "C'mon. That's it," Ellis encourages. Quinn stretches towards it; Ellis keeps up those delicious little thrusts and Quinn finally freezes, shudders, then shoots come, *hard*, spurting over and over onto the sheets, gasping with it while Ellis grabs his hips and fucks him, thrusts a few times then cries out. Quinn feels him spill hot in his ass, pumping again and again. He pulls out gently.

"Good boy, Quinn," he says. "What a tight little ass, sweet boy. Look how much you came for me. My god. I love watching my dick slide in and out of you." Ellis grabs him and pulls him down on the mattress into a spoon, then yanks the blankets up over them. Quinn snuggles in. Ellis holds Quinn's dick and toys with it some. Quinn hopes he doesn't get stiff again, because he'll want it and Ellis won't give it to him.

"We need to get up and go to dinner," Ellis tells him.

"Can't we stay in bed?" Quinn asks.

"No. You'd do nothing but stay in bed if I let you. You have your first day of school tomorrow. Are there things you need at your apartment?"

"Yeah," Quinn says.

"We'll stop there after dinner and pick them up."

"Do you want me to —" Quinn asks. He doesn't want to say it.

Ellis hugs him tighter. "I told you I wouldn't ask you to leave. But you're free to go whenever you want."

"I'd rather stay here," Quinn says quietly, thinking of how lonely his apartment can be. "I don't have class until eleven. Do we go hunting in the morning?"

"I don't work until eleven. Yes, we go hunting in the morning."

"I need my hunting stuff then, too." Quinn wiggles closer. His hair's probably in Ellis's mouth and he doesn't really care.

"I love to look at this in your breeches," Ellis says. He keeps playing with Quinn. If he keeps it up much longer Quinn's going to want to go again. "I love a big cock on a little twink."

Quinn turns and buries his head in Ellis's chest again. He smells so *good*, like leather and horses. "None of that, sweet boy," he says. "I'll go out to your car and get your suit, and you can dress for dinner for me."

Ellis leaves Quinn in bed and retrieves his gray pinstripe suit, blue bowtie, and blue socks. "Up, sweetheart," he says. "Time to get dressed." Quinn climbs very reluctantly out of the down nest. It's so warm and comfortable there, masses of pillows and soft fluffy comforter and sheets with a thread count higher than

Quinn's. "Can't we go to like, Princess and King for burgers sometime?" Quinn yawns. "Or like, watch a movie? Do we have to go out somewhere nice every night?"

"Compromise. Molly McPherson's is casual. You can dress like a frat boy. I'll dress like one too so we don't look mismatched, honey."

Ellis drives, of course. Ellis always drives. He opens Quinn's doors and holds his hand and generally hovers. It feels different; much more — Quinn doesn't have a word for it. Much more like Ellis is with him and he is with Ellis. Ellis keeps touching him: a hand in his, one on his back, steering him towards a table. He sits next to Quinn instead of across from him, and plays with his hand. "Tell me what you want to eat."

Quinn asks for an appetizer, salad, and a New York strip. Ellis orders for him.

"You're still growing," Ellis says fondly, not in the eye-rolling tone he usually uses about Quinn's food consumption. He strokes his cheek. "But you hardly have to shave, do you?"

Quinn jerks away. He hates to talk about that. "Not much," he says.

Ellis laughs a little. "Nothing to be embarrassed about, sweet boy."

Quinn feels a teensy bit better.

Ellis takes him home to get the things he needs to hunt and go to class tomorrow. "I get off work around six," he says. "Have a suit on and I'll take you to dinner."

"What if I don't wanna go to dinner?" Quinn asks. He likes to come home from school and play video games for a while. It clears his head.

"You don't have to," Ellis says gently. "Go home for awhile if you want. I'm sorry, I'll monopolize you if you let me."

"Maybe I'll come over," Quinn says. He'll think about it. If he's going to stay there all the time, maybe he'll bring some of his video game systems over, if he thinks Ellis won't throw a fit. He decides to risk it. "Daddy?" he asks.

"What is it, Q?" Ellis asks. Quinn can hear the indulgence in his voice, oh my god, Ellis will give him whatever he wants.

"Can I bring some of my game systems over? I like to play them when I get off school to chill out for a while."

"Of course you can, sweetheart."

"Thank you, Daddy." Quinn says sweetly, with lowered eyes. He kneels down and begins unplugging wires. Ellis stands behind him. Quinn's pretty sure Ellis watches his ass.

When they get back to Ellis's house, Ellis points Quinn towards a spare room with a dresser. "Put your clothes in there," he says. "It's empty. Then we can watch TV if you want."

Ellis puts on a documentary for a while. Quinn curls up with him. It feels so good to have someone to cuddle on. He's never had anyone to snuggle with, to wrap him up in a blanket and tuck him in, to bring him water. Ellis plays with his hair and kisses his head. His nannies didn't even treat him like this when he was small.

He doesn't pay any attention to the TV. He doesn't know what they watch. It's all Ellis, Ellis touching him, Ellis stroking his hair, Ellis asking if he wants anything.

Finally, Quinn excuses himself and goes up to the bedroom; the spare one where Ellis told him to put his clothes. Quietly, he shuts the door. He curls up on the bed. And as quietly as he can manage, Quinn begins to sob. It's as if something has broken inside him, almost permanently broken, and he's just noticed a yawning crack. Or he was falling, had always been falling, and the fall felt like solid ground until someone taught him to look beneath his feet. Nineteen years of loneliness crush down on him, a smothering kind of suffocation: the breath he took while he was drowning, the total quiet underwater, the people so blurry and far away. Now that he has begun to escape it, now that someone has yanked him up into the air, he's choking, he can't breathe because his lungs are full, and he can finally look at it, the seemingly endless depths he'd sunk into. The terror that it will envelop him again sends him shaking, choking, he can't get air, can't draw a breath. Quinn sobs. He sobs for where he's been and he sobs for what might happen. He keeps his face in the pillow so Ellis won't hear him.

But he must be gone a long time. Eventually the door opens. Ellis flips on the lamp. Quinn doesn't look up. "Baby boy?" Ellis asks. "You okay?"

Quinn just shakes his head into the down pillow. Even the guest room has too many pillows. He's long crawled under the navy blue velvet coverlet, into the soft sheets. He's only wearing a pair of his pajama pants and he's cold.

"You wanna tell me what's wrong?" Ellis sits on the bed and strokes his hair.

Quinn shakes his head again. But Ellis will drag it out of him. He'll bully and snark and use his Dom voice until Quinn tells him.

"Okay," Ellis says. "That's all right. You don't have to tell me. I wish you would, so I could help you fix it. But if you don't want to tell, that's all right too. C'mon. Why don't you come over into the big bed and I can tuck you in for real, baby boy? This isn't good for you on the day before class starts. I have some tea downstairs. Let me make you some lavender tea, Q. It'll help you sleep."

Quinn cries harder. His shoulders shake and he burrows under the covers. He wishes Ellis would go away. He's terrified Ellis will leave. Quinn may fly apart with the push-pull of it.

"Baby," Ellis says. Quinn can hear his sadness and it's so much worse, someone being sad over him. No one's ever sad about Quinn. He craves it and he hates it, because it will go away. He will have it, and he will lose it, and its leaving will feel worse than never having it at all.

"Will you trust me enough to tell me a little piece of it?" Ellis asks. "You don't have to say everything. Just a piece."

Quinn wants to tell so much. He wants to be held. The thought terrifies him. He can't recall the last time anyone held him when he cried. No, he can. Crispin's mom held him when he came out. He was sixteen.

"Come get in the big bed and let me tuck you in at least," Ellis coaxes. "Come on, sweet boy. Just do this one thing for me. Can you do that? Just one thing?"

Quinn shakes his head again.

"Okay," Ellis says. His voice stays low and calm. "That's okay too." He pulls the blankets down and slides in next to Quinn. Strong arms wrap around him. Ellis pulls Quinn into a spoon, a tight one: Quinn has balled up, and Ellis curls close. Ellis doesn't speak; he holds Quinn while he cries. Gradually, Quinn relaxes. Ellis's arms help him feel safe, help him forget the loneliness. He subsides gradually into sniffles, then turns and burrows into Ellis's chest.

"Do you want to talk about it now?" Ellis asks.

"I was a mistake," Quinn manages. "Everyone knows it. Everyone says it."

"Oh, honey," Ellis says. "You're not a mistake." He smooths Quinn's hair back, sweaty now from him crying so hard.

"Except I am. They didn't want me. They never wanted me. No one ever wants me."

"Quinn, you deserve to be wanted," Ellis says. "You deserve more than that."

Quinn doesn't say anything.

"You heard it so much they made you believe it, didn't they?" Ellis asks quietly. "Oh, Quinn. Oh, sweetheart. And I've been nice to you and you can't accept it. That's why you're up here crying."

"Sort of? I don't know?" Quinn ventures. "And you being nice made me realize how bad it really was and that sort of crashed in and then I got scared it would all go away and I'd have to know how bad it was but I'd have to go back to it anyway."

"You need to learn you're worth more than you think," Ellis says. "So it doesn't matter if you're here or somewhere else."

"How do I do that?" Quinn asks. "I'm not ... I don't know."

"We'll work on it so you do know," Ellis says. "Now it's bedtime, sweet boy. Come on. Daddy says time for a shower and then bed."

Ellis helps him up and leads Quinn into his bedroom. He's already changed the sheets. These are red, and just as soft. "Towels in the linen closet," Ellis says. "Use whatever product you want, I imagine we use about the same things."

The shower pounds down on Quinn's back. He makes it scalding, like he's washing away the sadness. When he steps out, he feels so much better. Something about someone else's shower, the shampoo that smells like Ellis, about the hairbrush, toothbrush, and towel carefully laid out for him. Quinn brushes out his hair, uses the toothbrush, wraps a towel around his waist, and goes back to the bedroom.

"Do you sleep in pajamas?" Ellis asks politely. "Or would you rather sleep naked?"

"I usually sleep naked, but if you'd rather ..." Quinn sort of trails off. Protocol baffles him.

"I'd like if you slept naked, Q. I'd like that a lot," Ellis says. "I usually do. The pajamas are for walking around the house." He pulls them off, folds them, and sets them on a chair; Quinn undoes his towel and hangs it on the hook in the bathroom. But oh god, the sight of Ellis naked, all six feet of him with that long hair tumbling down, plenty of chest hair, hair that starts at his chest and leads down, down to his belly button and then thickens before it blends into the neatly trimmed hair around his cock. Quinn can't help it. He rises again. Ellis laughs.

"Look at my boy. You can't help it, can you?"

Quinn shakes his head mutely.

"And I know you can't sleep in bed with me like that."

Quinn drops his eyes and shakes his head again.

"You little tease. Look at that thick cock. This is all because you were being a little brat and looking at me naked, weren't you?"

"Yessir," Quinn admits, eyes still downcast. God, he wants to play with himself so much.

"I wanted to go to sleep," Ellis says. "But now you're being a little tease. Be a good boy for me now, lie down and suck me while I finger you."

"How do you like your cock sucked, Daddy?" Quinn asks.

"Figure it out, boy."

"I wanna get it right."

Ellis laughs. "As long as you don't bite, I think it'll be right enough." Quinn lays down next to Ellis and takes the head of his cock in his mouth. Ellis is mostly soft, but he makes a pleased sound when Quinn begins suckling him into hardness. God, Quinn loves a cock getting hard in his mouth. He takes all of Ellis in again and again, fast, until he's stiff and gasping with pleasure. At the same time, Quinn feels Ellis's slippery fingers caressing his ass. "C'mon, sweet boy, open up for me," Ellis says. "Suck that cock and open up for me. That's it." Quinn holds his shaft and probes Ellis's narrow slit with his tongue, looking to see if he'll drip for him. Fingers slip into him and stroke his prostate; he moans around Ellis as he rubs it. "Good boy," Ellis says. "You like that? You love having your ass fingered. You're *still* so tight for me, aren't you?" Quinn sucks his head hard and jerks him, tonguing him, licking him while he keeps working Quinn, making him moan and stretching him. "Are you ready now, sweet boy? You tell me if you're ready."

"I'm so ready for your cock, Daddy," Quinn gasps. "Can I have it, please? Can I have your cock?"

"Mmm-hmm." He pauses. "But you're going to do all the work, sweet boy. Come sit in my lap."

Ellis kneels on the bed. Quinn starts to face him. "Uh-uh, baby. Turn around. You find that good spot and use my cock to make yourself come for me."

Quinn's always on his knees, his belly, or his back. Not like this. "Daddy? I've never done this," he says uncertainly.

"C'mere." Ellis helps Quinn position himself over his cock and lower himself down. There's the familiar stretching, breathing through the pleasurable pain of it. Then he's suddenly kneeling, Ellis's cock in his ass, nestled against the good spot. He gasps with it. His cock juts out. "You want Daddy to take care of that?" Ellis asks.

"Uh-huh, Daddy," Quinn says. Ellis holds him up with one arm, slicks one hand and grasps his cock. Quinn draws a sharp breath. This feels so goddamn good.

"Now move." Ellis sounds amused.

Slowly, reluctantly, Quinn raises himself on Ellis's cock, then lowers himself again. He gasps at the feeling. "That's it," Ellis encourages. "Do it again, sweet boy." Quinn does it a few more times. It feels so good, especially with Ellis jerking him. But as good as it feels, Quinn doesn't like it.

"Daddy? Can we do it another way?" Quinn asks.

"What's wrong, baby? Does it hurt?" Ellis asks, sounding alarmed. He slides Quinn off him. "Are you okay?"

"Yeah, I'm fine," Quinn says. He feels stupid. "I just didn't like it?" He looks down, still rock-hard.

"Quinn." Ellis tips his chin up so Quinn has to look at him. "Tell me what you need."

Quinn furrows his brow and feels even stupider. He really doesn't want to say it. He'll just sound dumb.

"Quinn." Warning creeps into Ellis's voice. "Tell Daddy what you need."

Quinn jerks his head away from Ellis's hand. "I want cuddled," he tells the bedspread. "But you don't wanna."

"Go get a towel," Ellis orders. "I just changed the sheets and I don't feel like doing it again right away. Then lie down with a pillow under your chest. Make sure that towel is under your cock."

Quinn grabs one and lays like Ellis asked. He feels Ellis behind him. "You want this so I can lie down and cuddle you?"

"Yes, Daddy," Quinn says in a quiet voice.

Ellis enters him gently and lays on top of him. It feels so good, that weight above him. Ellis nudges against that perfect spot, and Quinn arches his back up. He takes Quinn's hands out from under him and laces their fingers together. "That's it, sweet boy," he says in Quinn's ear. His cock moves right against that perfect spot. "Oh god, you're so tight for me. *Fuck* but you're tight. Is this what you needed, honey? Did you need Daddy to hold you like this?"

"Uh-huh," Quinn says. This is so *good.* His eyes half-shut with pleasure, Ellis stroking inside him; he'll come hard if Ellis doesn't stop. Quinn feels himself finally, finally relaxing. "I wanted you to cuddle me, Daddy. Can I come when I want to?"

"That depends." Ellis keeps thrusting. Their balls touch and oh god, Quinn loves that. "Are you going to come a lot? Tell Daddy how much you're going to come."

"I'll come so so much. I'm already all sticky from dripping, Daddy. Your cock feels so good. It's so big in me. Will you please please fuck me harder?"

Ohgod Ellis picks up the pace and Quinn arches up at him, begging. "Oh god, I'm gonna come in you, boy," Ellis manages. "You want me to come in you?"

Quinn's so close. "Fuck me *harder*, Daddy," he practically whines. "*Please* Daddy I wanna come too, I wanna come with your cock in my ass. I don't wanna wait until after, please Daddy. Then come in me so I can feel it. I love when you come hard in me." Ellis thrusts harder and hits that good spot; Quinn shudders under him and shoots onto the towel and against his own belly, pumping again and again.

"Good boy, come hard for Daddy. C'mon, sweet boy. That's what you needed. C'mon."

Quinn must drag Ellis along with him, because suddenly Ellis stiffens, freezes, and lets go hard in Quinn. Quinn can feel, in the last throes of his own climax, the hot rush of Ellis coming inside him. He whimpers at it and raises his ass again to take it.

When Ellis finishes, he makes Quinn raise himself up on his elbows some, turns his head and kisses him gently. "What a good boy you were," he says. "Don't think I didn't notice how much you wanted me to come in you. Such a sweet boy. Weren't you good for Daddy."

"I tried, Daddy." After Daddy pulls out and they clean up, Quinn cuddles into his chest again. "Daddy, I'm sorry that —"

"Shhhh," he says. "Never apologize over asking for what you need, or saying you don't like something. I don't want my boy doing things he doesn't like."

"It was okay?" That wasn't what Ellis had in mind for them hooking up. It worries him.

"It was fine, sweet boy." He laughs, and Quinn can feel the rumble in his chest. "Now Daddy says it's *really* bedtime. We have to get up early to hunt." He sets an alarm and flips off the lights.

Quinn turns and balls up like he does every night. Ellis wraps around him: an arm under his head, one reaching down to his belly. It slides down between his legs. "Can I hold you?" Ellis asks.

"Uh-huh," Quinn says. Ellis's hand wraps around his cock. He kisses the back of Quinn's neck. Quinn passes out cold almost immediately.

CHAPTER 6

Ellis wakes before the alarm; he always does. Quinn is still curled in a tight ball; Ellis has his hand on Quinn's belly, rather than his cock. But he set his alarm early on purpose. "Wake up, sweet boy," Ellis says. He slides his hand down. Quinn, of course, is already hard. "C'mon, baby Q, time to wake up." He toys with Quinn's cock a little, stroking it.

"Mmm, too early," Quinn murmurs.

"Wake up, baby boy," Ellis coaxes. He fondles Quinn some more. Quinn moves against his hand and opens his eyes. He smiles. "Daddy?" he asks.

"Flip on your back for me," Ellis says. This'll make Quinn sleepy again, and he'll need coffee, but he also probably needs it to act like a civil human being and not a slutty brat. Ellis doesn't feel like dealing with a raging hard-on at work after Quinn's teasing all morning. "You want Daddy to play with you before you get up?"

"Uh-huh," Quinn says sleepily. He turns on his back. Ellis spreads lube over Quinn's cock. He begins jerking him lightly, the way he likes. He pauses and rubs under his head. Quinn makes a pleased little sound and moves his hips. "Daddy?" he says. "Daddy, can I suck you? Please Daddy? I liked sucking you so much yesterday."

"Slutty little thing," Ellis says fondly. "You just woke up." But he's already stiff from playing with Quinn.

"Please can I lick you? I promise I'm good at it."

Ellis sighs. "I suppose I'll have to suck you too then, bratty boy." He grabs one of the washcloths on the table and wipes off Quinn's cock. It'll be delicious to have that cock in his mouth. "Aren't you a naughty boy to convince me to suck you off first thing?" But he says it kindly. Quinn can't take anything but kindness. He's too hurt. He'll mistake any kind of real punishment as rejection. They'll have to wait a long time to play that game.

Quinn flips around and takes in his whole hard cock at once, ohgod, and Ellis isn't small. He sucks and sucks, nuzzles the base of it, pauses, sucks a finger wet, and strokes his ass. Dear *god.* "What a good little slut for Daddy," Ellis manages. "Don't you suck cock so well."

Quinn slides back on him tight-lipped. He looks up with those big eyes. "Do I? Do I suck your cock right, Daddy?"

"Well, don't *stop,* sweet boy," Ellis scolds. He turns his attention to Quinn, rock-hard, god, he won't take long. Ellis sucks his head, and Quinn moans around him. He slides all the way down Quinn's cock, just to wet it, slides back, then sucks hard again and jerks him at the same time, swirling his tongue on his head. Quinn whimpers and bucks. He keeps taking all of Ellis in, sucking at him, licking him, and taking him in again, all the time fucking his ass up to the first knuckle. Ellis can't last, and he tenses on Quinn, who uses his other hand to cup his balls and stroke. Ellis shudders, thrusts, and spills down Quinn's throat. Quinn sucks him hard then, drawing everything out, then lessens his sucks until Ellis has finished.

He turns his attention back to Quinn. He drips so much; Ellis can taste the bitter-salt of precum in his mouth. Finally, he spreads Quinn's legs and moves his lips down to lick the tight little pucker there. Quinn moans with pleasure as Ellis jerks him and licks at the same time, then freezes and spurts hot on Ellis's hand and his own belly. Ellis keeps going; so does Quinn, pumping come over and over. Christ, so much of it. He finally calms, stops shuddering. Ellis cleans him off. He's wide-eyed.

Ellis laughs.

"No one ever did that, did they?"

Quinn shakes his head.

"Did that feel good, sweet boy?"

"Uh-huh, Daddy. You saw how much I came for you."

"You came so much for me, Q baby. I love when you come a lot."

Ellis brings him coffee. They dress. God. Quinn looks good in those breeches. Ellis forces him to eat breakfast, at least a protein bar, before they drive to the meet. "God, that was good this morning," Quinn says in the car. He's looked a little dazed ever since. "I can't tell you the last time I got blown."

Ellis cuts his eyes at him. "Really now?" he says in a neutral tone. Good god, Quinn's worse off than he thought. "When was the last time? I'm curious."

Quinn chews on his lip. He knows exactly when, Ellis realizes. He doesn't want to say. "High school. Calhoun."

That would have been more than a year ago. All the guys Quinn's had since then, and none of them have sucked him off. Jesus, his sex life really does play into every insecurity he has. "Sweet boy," Ellis says gently, "don't you think that's a little strange?"

"Not really," Quinn says. "I'm a little twink. People take me home to fuck me in the ass, not suck my dick, Ellis."

"Honey, you're not a little twink." Ellis glances at him. He's looking out the window as the trees flick past. "You're much more than that."

"I'm a cute little twink, Ellis. That's why *you* like me. I'm hot, I have a big dick, I'm fun in bed, and I call you 'Daddy', which for some fucked-up reason we both get off on. I'm just a fun game. It's okay. Just don't pretend it's more. It sucks when you do."

Ellis slams the brakes on and pulls over. They're driving on some country road in the middle of nowhere, all sweetgum and oak. Everything looks golden, misted; a perfect early morning. "No. Oh my god, honey, is that what you think is going on here?"

Quinn turns to him, eyes flat, like Ellis has never seen them.

"Isn't it?"

"Quinn," Ellis says as patiently as he can without panicking. "Tell me what happened. Tell me what we said that set you off. It was something. You were fine. You were happy this morning when you woke up. What did we say?"

"You made me realize the last time I got blown, Ellis, what the fuck do you think it was? And it made me remember exactly how much I matter, which is to say that I suck, about all I'm good for, honestly. I ride real well. And I suck real good dick. I don't do much else, and I don't much matter to anyone. I offered you the only rational explanation I can think of for what's going on here." He points at himself, then at Ellis, then back to himself again. "You can keep driving now. We're going to be late."

"Oh, sweet boy, no. No, no, no."

"Now you're going to give me some speech about how I'm better than all that and I matter and I'm important and blah blah. Yeah. I don't see the evidence."

Ellis puts the car back into gear. "We're going to hunt," he says calmly. "Then we're going to have a serious conversation about why it might be a good idea for you to talk to a psychiatrist or a therapist, baby boy."

"What?!" Quinn nearly shouts. He sits up straight in his seat "I'm not fucking crazy!"

"No one said you were," Ellis tells him. He's learned, through long, long years of practice, that acting calm when he's panicking can actually help him stop freaking out. "But you're engaging in enough disordered thinking that it's making you deeply unhappy. When I was — when I hit that point, I needed to talk to someone. I think you do too."

"You can't make me," Quinn says.

"I can't make you and I never would. But you're unhappy. Quinn, has no one ever suggested therapy to you before?"

"No," he snaps.

"Never?"

"No, because I don't — I don't need it."

"You know it's not because there's something wrong with

you. It's to help you feel better. You go to a psychiatrist the way you'd go to a regular doctor. Quinn, do you feel good?"

He doesn't answer.

Ellis breathes deeply and prays he's getting through. "I asked you a serious question, Q. Do you feel good? Do you wake up and feel okay every single day? Or do you think maybe a doctor might could help you feel better?" Quinn still doesn't answer. He just looks down. Stonewalling. Ellis starts the car and drives to the meet, hoping he got through; hoping the silence means Quinn is thinking. Quinn stays quiet all through the hunt, though he rides as well as ever and sticks close to Ellis. He hands his horse to the groom and gets back into Ellis's car. He slumps in the seat, but still buckles up. "So how do we find a psychiatrist?" he finally asks.

Ellis has to stop himself from breathing an enormous sigh of relief. "We call around," he says as casually as possible. "I know a few people."

He stays home from work, and keeps Quinn home from school, in hopes he can get Quinn an appointment. And he manages it: Ellis finds Quinn an appointment with the best doctor in Savannah for 3pm. "She had an opening," Ellis tells him. "You got lucky today, honey. Do you want me to go in with you?"

Quinn shakes his head.

"I don't mind."

"No. I have to do this by myself and I don't think I'll say some things if you're there."

So Ellis stays in the posh waiting room, filled with leather chairs and upscale magazines, *The New Yorker* and *The Atlantic*. Quinn emerges an hour later.

"We have to stop at the pharmacy," he says wearily, once they get in the car. "They called in the prescriptions but we have to pick them up."

"So what did she say?" Ellis asks cautiously.

"That I have dysthymia, which is basically chronic low-grade depression, and anxiety. She gave me some meds for both of them which she swore wouldn't make my dick not work. I said that was a dealbreaker."

Ellis laughs. "Yeah. You would say that, wouldn't you, honey?"

"No way am I taking something that makes my dick not work."

Ellis picks up Quinn's meds for him and pays for what his insurance doesn't. "You don't have to do that!" Quinn protests.

"Just let me," Ellis tells him.

"But —"

"Let me take care of you, Quinn. Just accept it."

"I'm trying, Daddy. I'm trying, but it's really hard."

"I know sweet boy," Ellis says. He takes Quinn's hand. Quinn lets him. "We'll get you feeling better, okay? We'll work on it together. We need you to know you're good and wonderful without someone telling you so. It has to come from inside instead of outside. The medication will help a lot, but you need to work hard, too."

"I'll try, Daddy," Quinn says.

"What do you need when we go home?" he asks patiently. "We already had lunch. Do you need something else to eat? Do you need a nap?"

"I'm not a toddler Ellis, god. I want to go home and play *The Legend of Zelda* or one of the *Final Fantasy* games. Do I need a nap? God."

Ellis lets the backtalk pass. Quinn has had a miserable day.

Later that afternoon, after Quinn has zoned out to video games, after Ellis has fed him some snacks and cuddled him on the couch, he's idly stroking Quinn's hip under the blanket when his hand accidentally brushes against Quinn's cock. He's unbelievably hard.

"Oh," Ellis says, making his voice soft. "Is there something my boy needs? All he has to do is ask." Ellis's breath quickens. "Why don't you start by going upstairs and taking your clothes off for me? If you want to, baby. Only if you want to."

He comes up to the bedroom to find Quinn, eyes downcast, biting his lip, that beautiful blond hair, a curtain over his face, slowly unbuttoning his shirt, folding it neatly, then setting it on the bed. He clasps his hands behind his back, sweet merciful Christ. The hair around his hard cock's just as blond as the hair on his head, trimmed short. "Do you like when I look at you?" Ellis asks gently.

Quinn nods.

"Little exhibitionist," Ellis says fondly. "Show Daddy how you play with that hard cock."

Quinn takes himself in his hand and rubs the underside of his head. Little shiny drops appear at his slit almost immediately; Quinn swipes them up and uses them to slick the spot he's petting. Ellis wants Quinn so much. He wants to pin him to the bed, that pink little ass in the air where he can see it.

"Does that feel good?"

"Uh-huh," Quinn says, finally finding his voice again. "It feels really good, Daddy. Look how much I'm dripping for you." Oh, Ellis can *see* how much he's dripping. He'd suck it off but his knees don't ever hit the ground.

"I think Daddy needs to fuck you, baby boy."

Quinn's lowered eyes flick up and then back down. "I wanna play, Daddy." Ellis *swears* he can see Quinn harden while he talks. This one likes to talk. He really, really likes to talk and he really, really likes to listen.

"Then I want my good boy to lay his head and chest down on the bed, feet on the floor, and keep playing with his cock. Do you want some lube? But you have to be good, Quinn. No doing it too much or I'll make you stop. Do you understand? I want you to last."

"Yes, Daddy," he says, so sweetly. He lies down, pushing the comforter out of his face, little ass in the air, slicks his cock wet the way he likes it, and jacks it so slowly. He whimpers a little with pleasure. Ellis finally takes himself out. He drops his pants part of the way, slicks himself, and lets himself rub his cock between Quinn's pink cheeks. He smacks his entrance with it; Quinn gasps and spreads his legs. "Good boy," Ellis says. "You like that?" He nuzzles his slick cock at Quinn's tight hole. He'd never enter him, not yet, but that little pucker feels so goddamn good on his head. Reluctantly, he withdraws and begins working his fingers inside Quinn, getting him ready. Quinn stands on his tiptoes and leans into him.

"Oh, Daddy, that feels so good. I love when you finger my ass. Please don't stop. Please please don't stop. Fuck me with your fingers? I'll be so good for you. I love when you slide your fingers in me and gimme more, I want *more*."

"How do we ask, sweet boy? Be polite."

"Please Daddy gimme more," Quinn begs. "*Please* Daddy."

A third finger, Quinn tenses on, then bucks and arches against. God, Ellis loves when he begs for it, the streams of words coming out of his mouth: mixtures of *fuck me* and *Daddy* and *please* and *I want it so bad, I'm so tight for you, look how hard my dick is, please I'll be so good.* Soon Ellis can't hold it any longer.

"You want it, baby boy?"

"*Please,* Daddy, please fuck me hard."

"You need it gentle first. I don't want to hurt you."

"I wanna take all of it."

"Shhh." Ellis watches as his dick disappears, as Quinn's tight little hole opens up for his cock and lets him slip inside, that pink little ass wiggling above it, *ohgod.* Soon he's rubbing that spot Quinn likes so much he's nearly shouting. "Keep playing with your cock for Daddy. Not too much. Just a little. Tell me how good it feels."

"I wanna come so bad, Daddy," Quinn moans.

Ellis starts slow, but picks up the pace quickly as Quinn keeps begging. Soon he's holding his hips, fucking him as hard as he dares while Quinn cries out and meets him thrust for thrust. "You gonna come for me? Show Daddy how much you come. I wanna see all that wet sticky come from your cock," Ellis manages. He won't last. His balls have already drawn up; they slap against Quinn's smaller ones.

"Daddy, hit the good spot, Daddy *please* rub against the good spot, please please please," Quinn begs. "I'll come so hard." Ellis thrusts deep and begins those slow, hard thrusts against Quinn's prostate. Quinn loses it, shaking and shuddering, freezing, curling up and then shuddering again. He pumps come onto his hand, presumably, and onto the mattress. Fuck all but this boy is messy about it. Those thrusts hit the underside of Ellis's cock and drag him along Quinn; he leans back, pushes deep, and pumps inside him, shooting hot into Quinn's tight ass. They both pant with the effort and drift down together, occasionally jerking with one more pump.

Ellis slides out of Quinn and finally pushes his pants off. They clean up everything — Quinn mostly came in his hand, and the sheets will live, thank god. "Look how much come," Ellis says. "What a good boy."

Quinn shrugs. "The more often I get off, the more I come."

Ellis smiles. "You'll come plenty in this house then. Do you wanna nap?"

"Yeah," Quinn says.

Ellis makes them a little down nest and cuddles Quinn up. Jesus god, his thighs are getting sticky. If Ellis thinks about it too much he'll get hard again. "You feel so good, sweet boy," he says. "We'll have you better soon. You wait. You'll feel so much better. After we nap we'll have dinner. I'll cook so we don't have to go out."

"Okay." Quinn yawns. Ellis finds Quinn's cock and plays with it a little. He can't help it. But then he just holds it. Quinn curls closer, and from his deep, even breathing, Ellis can tell he's asleep.

He makes pasta while Quinn zones out on video games. Ellis puts a hard no on playing again that night, saying they both have to wake up early, but he suspects Quinn jerks it in the shower. Oh well. Then he gets a delightful surprise in the morning as they dress. Quinn wanders in, half clothed, looking for his breeches — in a jockstrap.

Ellis's cock springs up.

"And why are you wearing that, sweetheart?" he asks.

"I'll be on horseback all day from 7 am until like, 5 in the afternoon," Quinn says.

"Come *here,* honey." Ellis spins him around and looks at his ass, that gorgeous, pert little ass, the straps running around his thighs, the perfect little package tucked up neat and tight. "I'm buying you more," he says.

"Ellis, I have plenty of them. I wear them like, every day."

"Are you *kidding* me?" He palms Quinn, who arches up to him shamelessly. No cup, so he can feel everything. "I should have set the alarm earlier for you baby boy, I'm so sorry. You need it in the mornings." Ellis glances at the clock. If they both grab protein bars and eat them in the car, they should have time. "How long would it take you?"

"Not long, Daddy," Quinn says. He looks up with those big, pleading eyes. "I'll go so quick."

"Take that off, get a towel, and lie down on the bed for me. On your side."

"Yes, Daddy." Quinn does what he's told. Ellis grabs the lube, fits himself around Quinn, and slicks him. "I need you to come for Daddy," he says. "Are you going to come hard for me?" He plays with Quinn the way he likes. First the underside of his head, then soft, light gliding all the way up and down his cock. He pauses and plays with his head again. Repeat, over and over until Quinn arches up and begs, then Ellis jerks him fast with more lube, slipping over his cock fast, until Quinn stiffens, freezes, makes a small noise and spills all over Ellis's hand. "That's it. Come for Daddy. C'mon. Keep going, sweet boy. I want it all out. Come on. I wanna see all that sticky come for me." Quinn bucks on him until he subsides into occasional shudders. Ellis kisses the back of his neck. "What a good boy to come so hard," he says. "Much better, isn't it?"

"Uh-huh, Daddy," Quinn says.

"Good boy." Ellis's dick throbs. "Now be sweet and get down on your knees for me."

Quinn's knees hit the floor. He holds his hands behind his back and looks up at Ellis with wide eyes. "Are you going to fuck my mouth now, Daddy?" he asks.

Jesus god Ellis has wanted this since he set eyes on that pretty blond hair. "I'll go slow at first so you get used to it, sweet boy," he says. Ellis grabs a fistful of Quinn's hair, and those gorgeous lips open and take him in, all of him at once, into his warm, wet mouth. Quinn sucks a little; he won't be able to do that for long, and Ellis lets himself enjoy it for a moment before he starts moving in and out, in and out of Quinn's mouth. "What a sweet boy with such a clever mouth," he says, picking up the pace. "That's it, baby. Take the whole thing. Take Daddy's cock. You gonna swallow all that come for me?" No, he's not. He definitely isn't. Oh god no he isn't. Ellis doesn't want him to. He pumps in and out of Quinn's mouth harder at the thought. His balls draw up. "That's it, baby. Daddy's so close. Come on, sweet boy. That's it —" Ellis shudders, pulls out of Quinn's mouth, and comes all over his lips. Quinn watches him, wide-eyed; he doesn't move or shy away. When Ellis finishes, he watches curiously to see what Quinn will do. He licks his lips off as much as he can, then swipes at his face with his arm.

"What a good boy," Ellis says, so pleased that he licked rather than acting disgusted, or wiping it all off at once. He kisses Quinn on the head. "Aren't you so good?"

Quinn shrugs. But Ellis sees him look down and smile a little, a small, private, happy smile. Ellis kisses him again. That's a good start.

They dress quickly and head out to hunt. Afterwards, Quinn hops in his car and drives off to class, presumably one or two on campus and then off to the stables. He says he'll come home around six, depending on traffic, about the same time as Ellis. Ellis has given him a key. He'll need a shower: lovely. Maybe he'll let Ellis do it for him.

CHAPTER 7

It goes along like this for a while. Quinn wakes up in the morning and Ellis gets him off. Sometimes they have sex. Sometimes Ellis jerks him off. Sometimes they suck each other and Quinn really likes that, sucking Ellis hard and his come shooting down Quinn's throat. Only then Ellis can't talk to him, and Quinn really, really likes when Ellis talks to him. Ellis calls him "honey" and "Q" all the time now, and when they're alone, "sweet boy" and "my boy" and "baby boy."

Quinn calls him "Daddy" now whenever no one else can hear. Sometimes he whispers it when they can and that always seems to make Ellis hard. When they go out, Ellis always touches him: steering him around with a hand on his back, holding his hand. He strokes Quinn's hair and touches his cheek; he sits next to Quinn instead of across from him and fusses with his tie. Most of Quinn's clothes migrate to Ellis's; Ellis takes to both buying him more and dressing him.And best of all, even better than the sex, Ellis fusses over him almost constantly. Baby Q, did you have breakfast? You need more sleep. Cuddle on the couch with me. Let me tuck you in. You need new riding gloves. Oh god, you fell off jumping today? Are you all right? I'll run to the pharmacy and get you aspirin. Speaking of medicine, are you taking yours? You seem better. Go to class. Have you done your homework? How was your exam? Tell me about your day, honey. I'll rub your back.

Ellis spanks him when he breaks the rules. It always makes him hard. Once he came, he actually *came*, after ten smacks on his ass. Ellis had made him clean it up and then spanked him again. He got hard a second time.

Quinn has never had another person, well, *care* so much. It stuns him. He started out suspicious, then he liked it, and now he luxuriates in it. He cuddles up to Ellis; he wraps around him. He begs for kisses.

He's also shameless about wanting sex, and wanting it all the time. Not like Ellis doesn't want it just as much. He just pretends not to.

Sometimes, cuddling on the couch, Quinn will throw Ellis his big-eyed baby deer look and say, "Daddy? Can I play with my cock?"

"And why would you want to do that?" Ellis asks one day. "We're watching a movie."

"Because it would feel good, Daddy."

"Mmm-hmm. You want to play with it? Come upstairs and strip." Quinn trots up happily and takes his clothes off, then folds them neatly and sets them on the chair. His cock stands straight out. "Oh, that won't do right now," Ellis says, gesturing at his dick. "You can't be hard. Cold shower, please."

"What, Daddy?" Quinn asks. He's getting better at controlling his mouth.

"Cold shower, Q. Now." Ellis uses the Dom voice. "And it better be cold."

Quinn purses his lips and furrows his brow and drags himself to the bathroom, showing in every single way possible that he does *not* want to do this. He shivers through a quick shower that leaves him soft, dries off, then returns. "What a good boy," Ellis practically purrs. "Such a good boy." He holds up a small, silicon ring. "Do you know what this is?"

"A cock ring?" Oh *fuck*. This'll either be really fun or really — not-fun.

"C'mere." Ellis takes Quinn's soft dick in his hand and slips it on. "You'll get hard. You'll stay hard. You'll stay hard longer and you'll have one of the best orgasms of your life." His hand lingers on Quinn, toying with him. "You said you wanted to play with your cock, baby boy? Now you can *really* play with it. You tell me if it starts to get tingly or numb or cold, okay? Lie down on your back, then, sweetheart." Ellis pins his wrists above his head with one hand. Quinn makes a small, pleased sound. Ellis kisses him hard, sucking his lips and nipping, then slipping his tongue into Quinn's mouth. "I love a naked little twink under me when I'm dressed," he says into Quinn's ear, moving over to trace it with his tongue. Quinn grinds on him; his cock hardens. And hardens more. Ellis stands suddenly and begins taking his clothes off. "Touch yourself," he orders. "I wanna see that big cock get harder."

Quinn rubs under his head as he watches Ellis unbutton his shirt, fold it, take off his T-shirt, fold it, then step out of his pants and underwear. God, he's getting hard, especially looking at Ellis's hard chest, knowing how good it'll feel on his, the way his chest hair will rub against Quinn's smooth body. His long hair will tickle Quinn's face again. He's sofuckinghard, oh my *god*, Quinn's never been this stiff in his life. He whimpers for Ellis to come back.

"Use words," Ellis tells him sternly.

"I want you on top of me again, Daddy," Quinn says. "Rub your cock on mine, I'm so hard."

But Ellis doesn't, oh *fuck*, instead he puts a pillow under Quinn, gets the lube, and looks critically at him. "I think my boy needs his cock sucked," he says silkily. "Do you need your cock sucked, honey?"

"Uh-huh," Quinn says. "Please, please Daddy. Please suck me off." Ellis begins licking the precum off his head, oh god it's so swollen, Quinn wants it so fucking much, and it feels like everything good in the world, especially when two of Ellis's slicked fingers start playing with his ass. They relax him then slide up to stroke his prostate; Quinn arches up to Ellis's mouth and moans. A third soon follows. They fuck him, in and out, while Ellis takes his whole cock in. He finally pops off. "You want my cock now?"

he asks, still fucking his fingers in Quinn's ass. "Tell me."

"Can I have your cock now, Daddy?" Quinn begs. "Please? I'll be so good. I can turn on my side or my knees or get up against the wall or —"

"Oh no, honey, I want you just like this. And you're going to get it so, so slowly."

Ellis takes his time slicking himself, then Quinn, which makes him moan and buck his hips. He gently slides into Quinn, then lies on top of him. His weight feels so good, and Quinn's cock tucks up neatly between them. God, it rubs Ellis's belly. "You want me to fuck you?" Ellis asks in his ear.

"Please fuck me, Daddy," Quinn whispers. He wraps his arms and legs around Ellis. The deep pressure of Ellis above him, inside him, cuddling around him — god, so good. When Ellis thrusts, he rubs a little bit against Quinn's cock and it feels amazing, him just barely grazing the good spot inside him and stroking at Quinn's stiff, stiff cock. Quinn begins to whimper, then moan, then finally shout, clawing Ellis's back with pleasure, biting his shoulders, begging him: *harder Daddy, fuck me faster Daddy, more Daddy more, I want your cock Daddy please please please give it to me oh god it's so good,* all sorts of nonsense, until he can't stand it, until he's right on the edge. He sinks his teeth hard into Ellis's shoulder and lets go, spurting come all over his own belly, all over Ellis, shouting with pleasure, Ellis cooing at him: *that's right baby, I'm right behind you sweet boy, Daddy's going to come so hard in your tight little ass, come hard for Daddy, love feeling that sticky come all over.* Then Ellis thrusts hard and pumps into him, and Quinn feels the hot spill inside him. He cries out again at it. Their bellies slip together; Quinn drifts down, down and shudders with the aftershocks of going so hard. Ellis holds him. He slides out, then slips the ring off Quinn's cock. Quinn almost yelps at his gentle touch after such a strong orgasm.

"Look at all that come," Ellis says. "You came so much for me, didn't you, sweet boy?" He kisses Quinn's stomach, oh god, right on all the stickiness, so fucking hot. "You always taste so good, do you know that?"

"I like that toy," Quinn manages.

"Mmm-hmm. I thought you would. Clean up and I'll cuddle you to sleep. I should turn your ass red for biting me, but I won't, since I never told you not to. But don't do it again. Disrespectful little thing." Ellis kisses him on the head and Quinn half-shuts his eyes with pleasure.

After that, Ellis puts the ring on him regularly. "You go fast," he says. "You're nineteen. I want to take longer."

One afternoon, Calhoun calls. "I haven't talked to you in *ages*," he says. "I'm coming home this weekend to see Gran. She's after me because I spend every free weekend driving up to Audie, and I can't keep blaming it on school anymore. You wanna hang out?"

"Sure," Quinn says. He's tried calling Calhoun a few times, but all he talks about is his super-awesome, super-perfect boyfriend, and Quinn gets sick of hearing about him, so he stopped calling. It sucks. He and Calhoun used to be best friends. That "used to" hurts more than anything. He hasn't told Calhoun about Ellis. Calhoun never asked if he's seeing anyone, and he couldn't find the right words to tell him, so it just never came up.

So, on Saturday night he shows up at Calhoun's house for dinner. Of course his Gran is there, and she fusses over Quinn. But she knows everything about everyone. If Savannah is a hive, Gran's the queen bee. So when Calhoun's phone inevitably rings, and he inevitably says, "Excuse me, I have to take this. Study group," (it's Audie), Gran purses her lips.

"So who are you seeing, Quinn Rutledge?" Gran asks.

"No one," he immediately says, and throws her baby-deer eyes.

Baby-deer eyes do not work on Gran. "Huh," she says. "Not what I heard."

"What did you hear?" he asks.

"You're seeing someone much older than you."

"I might be," he hedges. What the fuck. "His name is Ellis Ashford. He's an architect." And all at once he just told the entire greater Savannah area.

"Interesting." Gran says. "Boy your age. I remember his father, Livingston."

"What about him?" Quinn asks. He hadn't even known Ellis's dad's name, he realizes, suddenly. He knows his mother's. Ellis knows his parents'.

"You don't know?"

"Know what?" Quinn asks.

"Mmm, interesting," Gran says.

Calhoun comes back. Quinn thinks about asking Ellis, but decides not to. If Ellis wanted him to know, he'd have said something. But he files it away.

His meds start to work. He stops suspecting Ellis just wants him around for sex. He stops suspecting people don't want him around at all, in fact. Sometimes, when they go hunting, Quinn leaves Ellis alone and rides around and talks to people. He says hello to Henry's mother, who seems delighted to talk to him. She asks about the "older man" he's seeing. Quinn knows it's just for gossip, but he tells her his name is Ellis Ashford, he's an architect with the Melbourne Firm, he collects antiques. Went to Emory and Duke. Oh, he's thirty-eight, ma'am, had his birthday in September. He smiles when he says Ellis's age, which is double his and he knows it. Mrs. Culliver raises an eyebrow and asks where they met.

"Here," he says. "Out hunting. We were going hunting together every morning."

He turns the conversation and asks about Henry and Wills. So now the greater Savannah gossip mill knows *all* about Ellis, not just that he exists. As if they didn't before. But now they know his exact age, as compared to Quinn's exact age, and the doubling makes it even more delicious. Gran will be all over this one.

Most of his other friends have gone back to school, or don't hunt once cub-hunting's over and the real season begins. Lucky and Thor can't be bothered to dress up. Crispin hates to ride, and has since they were kids. Delia and Isabel like to, but neither of them have horses right now. He calls up Delia one day and asks if she'd like to go with him. "Oh, only if Isa can come too," she says. "I hate to leave her out. You know how much she loves to ride."

So Quinn has *both* his other horses trailered over, one Saturday morning. Isa and Delia are fearless riders, so he lets them pick; Delia takes the bay thoroughbred mare he uses for dressage, Zelda, and Isabel takes his big-boned eventing gelding, Lucifer. Delia remembers Ellis; they introduce him to Isabel, who's super sweet but kind of a space cadet. She can ride like a demon, though, has since they were kids. Plus she looks adorable in her riding habit, all her strawberry blond hair neatly tied up, and boosted on top of gigantic Lucifer. Quinn isn't into girls, but if he were, he'd probably go for Isa. He tells her that and she giggles.

Delia rolls her eyes at her cousin. "You're gay. Stop flirting with her."

Isabel sticks her tongue out. "You're just jealous."

They have a fun ride; the girls seem to enjoy Ellis and he seems to like having the girls along. Afterwards, on the car ride home, he says so. "It was nice seeing Delia and Isabel," he says. "I like seeing you reaching out to your friends, Quinn."

"What d'you mean?" Quinn asks. He loosens his stock tie. God, he hates those things.

"You never used to. You went drinking with them before we were together, then you never saw them. Now you're actively calling them, and, to do things other than get plowed. It's good for you."

Quinn blinks slowly at Ellis. "Do you mean I'm being a good boy?" he asks sweetly.

Ellis rolls his eyes. "You're incorrigible, child."

Quinn sticks out his lower lip, just a little. "I was just *asking*, Daddy."

"Behave, sweetheart. You're teasing." Daddy strokes his cheek.

Quinn smirks. "I can think of *much* more effective ways of teasing, Daddy."

"Don't be a little slut, Q."

"You like when I'm a little slut."

"Not when I'm trying to drive, I don't. Save it. Bad enough you're hard in those breeches. Brat."

"I didn't make you look, Daddy."

"You didn't have to. You knew I would. And don't you dare touch it or even ask permission to."

"Maybe I'll touch it anyway. It's my cock."

"Maybe I'll punish you when you get home."

Quinn slides his hand down between his legs and finds the sweet spot behind his head. "This feels *good*, Daddy."

Daddy keeps glancing over. "Dammit, brat, quit it."

"But I like playing with it. I like when you watch me play with it, too."

"Every minute you do it now, is one day you don't get off when you wake up."

Fuck. Quinn likes his morning sex. "I'll just jerk off in the shower."

"You'll do no such thing."

"How're you going to stop me?"

"I'll watch you shower."

Quinn smirks. "You try that and see how it works out for you."

Ellis seems close to pleading. Quinn's winning. Ellis is probably going to turn his ass red for this when they get home. "And anyway," Quinn adds, "you like playing with me in the morning."

"But I have more self-control, brat. Something I've been remiss in teaching you." Ellis regards him carefully. "That starts today, I think."

Quinn's stomach flips.

He's right: when they get home, he's sent upstairs to strip and grab his ankles. Count ten. Ellis turns his ass bright red. But when he finishes, and Quinn's rock hard, big-eyed, pouty-lipped, looking a little sad — all intentional — Ellis tells him to put his clothes back on.

Quinn blinks a few times. "Daddy?" he says.

"Hmmm?" he asks.

"Daddy, I'm so hard. I need to play," Quinn tells him, and

shoots him the baby-deer eyes.

"Playing is for good boys," he informs Quinn. "You just misbehaved."

"Can I play with my own cock, then, Daddy?"

"No. You cannot. Put your clothes on and behave yourself, please. Do you want to come cuddle on the couch and watch a movie?"

"No," Quinn says, as un-sulkily as possible. "I'm just going to stay up here and read."

Godfuckingdammit. He's *so fucking hard*. And his ass hurts. So he dresses, stretches out on the bed, and reads for a while. But his cock's pressed against the bed, and it feels *good*. This isn't helping. He doesn't want to sit or lay on his back because it'll hurt his ass.

Fuck everything, this sucks.

"If you're done sulking, you can come down for dinner," Ellis calls eventually.

"I can't sit in a fucking chair!" Quinn yells back.

"Quinn Rutledge! Get your ass down here!" Ellis shouts.

Great. Now he said "fuck."

Quinn presents himself in the kitchen, the autumn sun slanting down through the windows. "Tell me what word you just used, Q," Ellis says.

He won't fall for that. Quinn shakes his head.

"Why not, honey?" Ellis asks.

"It's a trick to get me to say it again so you can punish me," Quinn says. "So I'm not going to say it. We both know what I said and I'm not sorry. My ass hurts and I can't sit down, so no, I can't 'come down for dinner,' Ellis. God."

Ellis sighs. "Quinn," he says. "Do you really think I'd make you say it again just so I could punish you? Sit down and eat, baby boy."

"I'm gonna go take a shower and see if maybe my ass doesn't hurt so much afterwards," he says.

"You never complained about it before," Ellis points out. "C'mon, honey. I made you some dinner, love."

"Yeah, well, maybe you didn't do it as hard."

"I didn't do it any harder than I always do."

"Maybe the endorphins afterward usually take care of it, then!" Quinn stomps upstairs and hops in the shower. He turns the water on scalding hot, which does nothing to make his ass feel any better, but he still stays there for a very long time.

When he finally gets out, Ellis is waiting. "Are you finished?" he asks.

"Clearly I've finished in the shower," Quinn says. He hitches his towel up. White and fluffy, of course, like everything else up here.

"I didn't mean with the shower."

"Then I don't know what you're talking about."

"Quinn, baby. Stop and calm down. Take deep breaths and tell me why you're so mad."

Sometimes, Quinn hates when Ellis acts so reasonable. "I'm *fine*," he snaps.

"Quinn. Nothing will get better until you tell me why you're angry. You were teasing and went too far. I called you on it. You aren't used to facing the consequences of your actions."

"I was playing a *game* and you were playing a *game* and you changed the rules!" Quinn snaps. He pulls on his towel again, then pauses, partially unwraps it, and tightens it. So embarrassing to have this argument in a goddamn towel.

Ellis looks at him, level. "You think this is a game?" he asks.

"What?" Quinn's confused.

"All of this. You think this is one big game we play?"

Quinn feels even more confused. "It's a sex thing. It's fun. Because I let you play the game with me, you fuss over me and treat me really well and everything. And it's really great. I really love it. But yeah, it's a game."

Ellis suddenly looks stricken, like Quinn slapped him or told him to fuck off or threatened to leave or something. "What?" he asks, panicking suddenly, though he isn't quite sure why. "What did I say?"

"Quinn," Ellis says. "I'm in love with you."

Neither of them has ever said that word to the other. No one's ever said that word to Quinn. He doesn't know what to say so he doesn't say anything.

"Quinn?" Ellis asks.

"I don't — I mean —"

"You don't love me?"

"No, I mean, I don't — I don't know!" he finally yells. "I've never even had a boyfriend! My parents don't love me! My brothers and sister don't love me! I don't know if my friends love me or not! I don't even know what it fucking *feels* like! So *I don't know*, okay? I don't even know what it *means*."

Ellis takes a deep breath. "Okay," he says. "Okay. We'll figure that out together for you, then, all right?"

"And how the blue fuck are we going to do that, Ellis?" Quinn asks. He feels close to tears and doesn't know why.

"Is there anyone in the whole world you can think of that you know you love? And by 'love,' I mean, you'd do something for them that might hurt you — or *would* hurt you — even though you know it would help them or they needed it?"

Quinn thinks. "Delia. Calhoun. Isa. Henry."

"Okay," Ellis says. He sounds very patient. "That's what love means. When you're willing to give away something even though it hurts you." He pauses. "Do you feel that way about me? Like, if I know you want coffee, I'll go down and get it for you, even if I'd rather stay sitting. That's a little example. A big one is not freaking out when the person you love doesn't know if they love you, but instead putting your feelings aside, even though you hurt very much, and trying to help them figure it out."

Does he feel that way about Ellis? Quinn really really wants to say this is just fun, he doesn't feel that way, because it's so much easier and less messy and much, much less frightening.

He looks at Ellis. He knows his eyes are probably wide and probably scared. He imagines Ellis holding him, and kissing him, and showing him in every way he can, that he cares. Quinn can't imagine losing Ellis. Quinn would hurt anyone who tried to hurt Ellis. He'd give Ellis whatever he asked for. Even when he was mad.

"I think I love you too," Quinn says after a while, and his voice shakes. He's too far gone to care. "But what if you stop loving me all of a sudden?"

"Love doesn't work that way."

"It will if I fuck up." Quinn swipes a tear off his cheek. "Like today. If I do that too much."

"What did I tell you at the very beginning? You never have to leave as long as you keep trying."

"But what if I'm really trying, and you think I'm not, and —"

"Quinn, honey." Ellis's voice sounds patient and kind again. "Shhh. Take a deep breath. Lie down and let me hold you for a while, okay?"

"But I'm not wearing anything."

"I think we can manage to lie down for once and not do anything," Ellis says. "Just let me hold you for a little while, baby."

Ellis pulls off his shirt and his jeans. "You never get into bed with clothes on," he reminds Quinn. "Barbaric." Quinn burrows into his chest. He smells so good, that familiar leather-and-horse scent. Ellis pulls the down comforter over them, and Quinn feels so cozy, warm and comfortable; so comforted suddenly. He is in bed with someone he loves. This someone loves him. Quinn closes his eyes and just lets himself feel it.

Of course, cuddled against Ellis in bed, tangled against him, the inevitable eventually happens. Ellis laughs gently. "You can't help it, sweet boy, can you?"

"No," Quinn says. He feels himself flush. But it would feel so good. He'd feel so taken care of and ... well, loved. In a good way, not the way he used to; the times he'd stand in his shower until his skin turned red.

Ellis kisses him on the head. "God help me. Can I, baby boy?"

"Oh, Daddy, please, would you?" Quinn begs.

Ellis's big hand closes over his cock, and Quinn practically purrs with pleasure. "Such a simple thing to give you, sweet boy," he says. "Tell Daddy what you want."

"Cuddle me?" Quinn says.

Ellis seems to think for a second. "I can do that, but you tell me if you don't like it, okay, baby?"

"Okay, Daddy," Quinn says.

Ellis pulls the blankets down, grabs the lube, kisses down to Quinn's cock, and opens him up while he sucks. Quinn whines and moans and bucks at the warm mouth working his cock and Ellis's slicked fingers fucking him. When he's begging and whimpering, Ellis sits up, legs folded. "C'mere, Q baby, sit on my cock for me," he coaxes. "Face me. Not like last time."

Reluctantly, because he'll probably hate it, Quinn straddles Ellis, who helps him lower himself through the familiar pleasure-pain of opening up, of his muscles stretching for Ellis's cock. "You're doing so good," he says. "You're doing so good for Daddy. That's right, sweet boy. C'mon. Just a little more." Quinn sighs when Ellis has settled inside him; he doesn't *quite* hit the right spot, but it's good.

"Wrap your legs around me," Ellis says. "C'mon, sweet boy." Their height difference, and Quinn's longer legs compared to his torso, leaves him only slightly taller. Ellis holds him tight in his strong arms. Quinn nuzzles in and twines his arms tightly around Ellis's neck.

"There, baby." Ellis says. "How's that?"

Quinn nuzzles into his shoulder and closes his eyes. Ellis laughs a little. "Move your hips for Daddy now," he coaxes. "Make yourself feel good, baby." Quinn begins swiveling his hips while Ellis holds him; Ellis's long hours, in the gym and on horseback, are paying off. Quinn's own time in the saddle has made him limber, and, *ohgod* when he moves, he can make Ellis's cock rub against his prostate. Ellis groans with pleasure. Then, shockingly, he reaches down with both hands and *lifts* Quinn's ass, fucking him up and down. "So light, baby," he says. "You're such a little thing."

"I'm not that little!" Quinn flares.

"You are compared to me, baby twink. Hush for Daddy and let me fuck your tight ass." He lifts Quinn again and again, in a regular rhythm, gasping with pleasure. Quinn unwraps his legs, puts his knees on the bed, clings to Ellis, and begins fucking him hard and deep, hips circling at the same time. He whimpers and has to stop himself from biting. Ellis bites him instead. “That’s it, sweet boy. What a good boy to ride my cock. You like that? You like riding me like your horse? Bet that feels so good in your tight little ass. Imma come so hard in that ass. You want Daddy to come?”

Quinn isn’t close but he nods. “Uh-huh, Daddy. Wanna feel you come in me. I love feeling your hot come in me.” He moves on Daddy faster. “Fill me up, Daddy? Please? I wanna feel you come. Will you come a lot?”

“Ohgod, baby boy, don’t you dare stop. Keep going for Daddy. Lemme feel that tight little ass. Oh*fuck* —” Ellis yanks Quinn down on him, pulls him as close as he can, thrusts up into him and lets go hard, shooting hot into Quinn again and again. Quinn swivels on him and rides it. *Love it Daddy come so hard for me your come’s so good in my ass Daddy Daddy Daddy Daddy* and on and on. When Ellis finishes, he takes Quinn’s face in both hands and kisses him, long and slow, still inside him.

“Here, sweet boy,” he says. “Climb off me and we’ll take care of you.”

“I feel so *empty,* though,” Quinn complains. He knows Ellis is going to jerk him and it’s going to feel so good, but he wants to come with his ass full.

Ellis smiles. “I was going to save it for later. But… ” He reaches into the side drawer, “I got you another present.” A slim anal plug, clearly meant to slide into an ass and stay there. “You want this while I jerk you off?”

“Yesplease Daddy,” Quinn says eagerly.

Ellis slides it inside him. Quinn can feel it shift some when he moves, and he loves it. Ellis throws a towel down in front of Quinn and spoons him. “How close are you, sweet boy?”

Quinn wiggles against the plug. “Close-ish, Daddy.”

“What’ll make you go?”

“If you hold me and play with my cock and talk to me.”

“I think I can do that, baby Q.” Ellis slicks him luxuriously and rubs under his head. "There it is, baby, I know that's your favorite spot. Tell Daddy how much you like it."

"I love when you touch me there, Daddy. That's where I like to touch myself."

"I know you do, sweet boy." He begins jerking Quinn slowly, pausing to play with his head, then jerking him again until Quinn bucks and arches and begs. "Ask for it nicely," Ellis warns indulgently. "You know how to ask."

"Please let me come, Daddy. Please let me come hard."

Ellis jacks him quicker, slipping over his cock faster and faster. Quinn's toes curl up; he strains toward Ellis's hand and he knows he's saying nonsense and he doesn't care, he's so close and his ass feels full and he's going to go, he's going to spill, and then he's pumping come all over Ellis's hand while Ellis coos at him. *That's it baby boy, come for Daddy. Come hard for Daddy, I wanna see all that hot sticky come all over my hand. You can do it. C'mon love.* Quinn eventually subsides into fluttering shudders. Ellis wipes his hand off and cleans everything up. Then he snuggles Quinn close.

"Do you feel better now?" he asks gently.

Quinn nods. He doesn't trust his voice.

"Do you understand that I love you? You don't have to say it back. I know you love me. I know it's scary right now and it's okay not to say it for a while. Love means giving people space when they need it."

"I do, but I think I need space because it's scary," Quinn says in a rush.

Ellis plays with his hair. "You know, you never used to talk to me. Not really talk. You'd run your mouth but you never said anything. You talk now, like you think you have something important to say. That makes me happy, Quinn."

"You're the first person who ever realized I never said anything," Quinn says. He's carried that one around for a long time and he's never told anyone, never voiced it. "Everyone mistakes talking for saying something. But it isn't the same." He curls up. "I never had anyone, other than Calhoun and once in a while

Henry, who actually listened."

"Calhoun sounds like a good friend."

"I miss him a lot when he's in Charleston. Not the hooking up. Just being around. We've been best friends since kindergarten. He's, like, the nicest person in the world. But he has this super-hot and super-awesome boyfriend he's obsessed with now, so we don't talk like we used to."

"You should go see him."

Quinn shrugs. "I will soon. Everyone'll be home for like, a week, for Thanksgiving. I think people wanna go to Tybee for a night. Friday, and maybe Saturday while our moms shop. Most of us have off Monday too and the whole week before."

"That'll be fun for you."

"Yeah, except the hell of Thanksgiving beforehand." Just the thought of it makes him cuddle closer to Ellis.

"It'll only be a few hours."

"That's bad enough."

He feels Ellis tense. "I know how you feel, baby."

CHAPTER 8

Ellis and Quinn wake together on Thanksgiving morning. Ellis gets Quinn off as usual: delicious. Fucks him on his belly with a pillow under his chest while Quinn calls him Daddy, begs for more of his cock, then comes hard with Ellis's cock in his ass, Ellis telling him come for me baby Q, I wanna see my boy come as much as he can, that's it, Daddy loves it when his boy comes so much. He lays out Quinn's suit, a checked three-piece with a gray tie. Quinn has sworn that yes, his family dresses for Thanksgiving dinner. Ellis pulls on a button-down, khakis and a sweater — total frat boy — kisses Quinn, says he has to go start the turkey for his mother, and leaves.

Quinn isn't expected until 3:00 pm. He sits alone and plays video games, numbingly, until 1:30 in the afternoon. Then he dresses, makes sure he looks impeccable, and drives himself out to the family farm, down I-16, out an exit and down the winding roads to a place not far from Henry's, on the far outskirts of Savannah. It has a goddamn name: Charleton Place, formerly owned by the Charleton family, but in Quinn's family for god knows how long. He drives up the long, winding, pebbled drive lined with live oaks, to the huge house with the double staircase out front, god, cliché upon cliché, the thing even has fucking columns. Of-fucking-course, he's the last one there; all his brothers' and sister's and parents' cars neatly line up in a row: Alexander and Thomas both have high-end Mercedes minivans.

Tristan, of course keeps a Porsche; he fucking loves fast cars. Darcy, his two-years-older sister, the precious, precious girl, who gets a new car whenever she wants it, is in a Land Rover right now. His parents both drive Teslas because his mother's on some green kick.

Quinn straightens his suit, prays the kids won't gum it up with their greasy little paws, and climbs the stairs into the house. He rings the bell; they keep it locked and he doesn't have a key... not to the front. Marigold, his five-years-older brother Tristan's girlfriend, answers the door. "Hi, Quinn!" she says perkily, her blond hair swaying. She and Quinn have approximately the same haircut, though hers is bleached like a Fox News anchor, that weird shade of green-blond. "You're just in time for dinner!"

Everyone's seated in the formal dining room already. Quinn checks his watch. He's arrived fifteen minutes early. Quinn hates this room: all staid portraits of deceased Rutledges, shiny, shiny wood no one can touch for fear of fingerprints, knickknacks owned by the illustrious dead.

The kids sit at the actual table. When Quinn was small, his parents banished them to a kids' table in the kitchen, but *grandkids* and all that, so the brats have to eat with them. Quinn actually really likes kids in general. But both Alexander's and Thomas's kids are grade-A *brats.* Trey (Alexander III) and Tommy (Thomas Jr.) whine for whatever they want, and they get it. Alexander's Johnny cries all the time. He's three, so you can sort of forgive that, but it's *all the goddamn time.* Five-year-old Archie — who the fuck names their kid Archibald? Apparently his brother Thomas does — screams and lies and speaks in a volume usually reserved for those who have just exited a Metallica concert. He actually likes his only niece, Liliana. She's a year old and has no personality other than drooling. Though he hasn't seen her since Easter, so who the fuck knows.

There's a general round of hellos. The Rutledges, at least this branch, do not hug. His parents sit at opposite ends of the table: his father, blond as Quinn, at the head; his mother, black-haired, through the judicious application of dye, at the foot. Five kids, and only Quinn got the Rutledge hair. Everyone sort of resents him for that. You'd think they'd feel grateful, but apparently it made the oops thing even worse.

They sit. Everyone talks about the kids. What are they doing? How are they doing in school — as if you could call what everyone but Tommy does, school: Christ, none of the rest have even hit kindergarten. Glorified daycare. Why aren't their *mothers* taking care of them, at least part of the time, since they claim to be "stay-at-home-moms"? Quinn doesn't want to be judgy but *Jesus*, when you put your kid in "school" for seven hours a day from age two on ...

What is everyone else doing?

Mother goes on and on and on about the goddamn Garden Club. She's president. Their big Christmas party is at The Narrows next weekend and it's soooooo stressful and oh my god. They had all better show up, unless they're dead.

Father talks about the miserable, miserable life of a corporate CEO. The hell of private jets. Flying across time zones. Incompetent underlings. Firing people. A lot about firing people.

Alexander, of course, is a fucking doctor and everyone loves Alexander because he's a goddamn heart surgeon and please spare us vivid descriptions of medical procedures while Quinn attempts to eat meat, thanks. Thomas drones on about finance, boring boring boring. Their wives tweet about Junior League. They both claim to be stay-at-home moms, but have nannies and shop and do lunch all the damn time. Tristan, who's seminormal, still attends graduate school for public health, which his parents find mildly embarrassing. Darcy, oh, they *bought* Darcy's way into Brown, where she has no particular major right now but she's figuring it out and she flips her perfect, perfect black hair and blinks her perfect, perfect black eyes and everyone loves her.

Then they round on Quinn.

"How's school, Quinn?" his mother asks. She tucks back her fake black hair.

"Good. I have all A's this semester." This he can manage.

They spend some time asking about his horses: how many does he have right now again? What are their names? What's he do with them again?

Quinn's waiting for it.

"I heard you're seeing an older man," his mother says.

Oh *fuck.* Here it comes. His mother gossips with the best of them. Quinn sits up straighter and dabs at his mouth with his napkin. Welcome to the Spanish fucking Inquisition.

"Yeah, his name is Ellis Ashford? He did Thurston and St. Albert's, and Duke for architecture. He's a partner with the Melbourne Firm." Quinn knows this sounds very impressive — not that Ellis isn't impressive — but when you stack it up like that, he sounds pretty spectacular.

"Um. I heard he's like, super older than you?" Alexander's wife, Lily says. She's a raging bitch and also loves to talk talk talk about everyone, including, apparently, her own goddamn family.

"He's older than me, yeah." Quinn keeps to a straight face and evasive answers. Even the dead people on the walls look accusatory.

"How old is he?" Quinn's father asks.

"In his thirties," Quinn says. True enough without directly answering the question.

"Um, seriously?" Alexander asks. He's the oldest of them at twenty-eight.

"Problem?" Quinn asks. He smiles at his brother.

"Isn't that, like, way too old for you?" Darcy asks. "That's kind of icky, Quinn." Darcy hates him.

"I don't think so, no," Quinn says. He decides to continue eating as if this conversation utterly bores him. Candied yams. Green beans. Turkey. Biscuits. Oyster casserole. Everything cooked downstairs by other people, brought to the table, set by other people. Other people will clear the table and other people will wash the china and polish the fucking silver. What a waste for a bunch of people who truthfully don't like each other very much at all.

"I think he's too old for you," Thomas chimes in.

"Your opinion wasn't requested," Quinn says smoothly.

"A guy that age with someone your age is only interested in one thing." Thomas crosses his arms.

"Maybe that's all I'm interested in," Quinn tells him, just to shock everyone at the goddamn table. "Anyway, I met him out fox-hunting, so he's not disreputable." He carefully breaks off a piece of biscuit, butters it, and pops it in his mouth. Manners, manners, manners.

"Quinn Rutledge!" His mother draws in a breath the way she's done since he was small and exasperated her at every turn. Since his entire *existence* exasperated her, which is to say, since Quinn existed as a clump of cells. "There are children present!"

"Who have no damn idea what we're talking about, Mother," Quinn says.

"What are you talking about, Quinn?" Tommy asks. It pisses him off that the kid never calls him "uncle." He *was* twelve when Tommy was born, but still: he's nineteen now. Show some goddamn respect.

"Ask your daddy after dinner, he brought up the topic," Quinn tells him.

"Quinn, if you can't behave —" his mother starts. His father never says anything.

"I'm behaving fine, Mother." Quinn keeps eating. He figures this is his best tactic. He isn't hungry in the least.

She sniffs. "Well, at least you stopped all that partying, I hear."

"From whom did you hear that, Mother?" Quinn asks politely.

She waves her hand. "People."

"Those people do love to talk, don't they?" he says blandly.

"Well, I don't think you should see this man anymore," she says.

"Excuse me?" Quinn asks.

"It's indecent."

"Could you explain that, Mother?" Quinn asks in his sweet voice. "I'm not sure I understand how Ellis is indecent."

She stutters, starts, stops, shuts her mouth.

"You know exactly what she means," Alexander huffs.

"Maybe she could try: 'Hey Quinn, does he make you happy? Is he nice to you? Does he treat you well and is he a good guy?'"

"I don't think that's relevant to the discussion," his mother snaps.

Quinn gives up. He always does.

He manages to escape after another hour and speeds back to Ellis's. Of course, Ellis isn't home yet. So he sits cross-legged on the expensive Persian rug, back to the plush gold couch, and turns on his PlayStation. Ellis returns home around nine, to find him shirtless in front of the TV, legs still crossed, playing Grand Theft Auto and blowing up everything.

Ellis looks at him for a moment. "You seem upset," he says mildly.

"My family tends to do that to me."

"Do you want to talk about it?"

"No. I hope your mother was well," he says politely.

"She was. She asked all about you." Ellis clenches his jaw.

Quinn snorts. "Your mother wasn't the only one giving you the third degree."

"What was the verdict in your house?"

"You're a lecherous fuck."

"Well, you're looking at a sugar daddy trying to rescue you from your waywardness."

"That's not far off." Quinn dies and restarts. "Your mother is a wise woman."

"Quinn. You know it's more than that."

"Mmm-hmm." He cruises around and looks for people to kill. That's the best way to get the cops to chase you. Then you can run from them.

Ellis sits on the floor and fits himself next to Quinn. "C'mon upstairs and take a shower. Did you hang your suit up like a good boy?"

"I'm not in the mood, Ellis."

"For which part, Q?"

"Any of it."

"Can I sit here?"

"Rather be left alone."

"I'm going to read on the couch. Is that all right?"

Quinn appreciates that Ellis respects his need for space in his own goddamn house. "I don't care. I'm going to bed anyway. We're going to Tybee tomorrow for two nights."

Ellis's eyebrows knit. "When were you planning on telling me that?" He sounds annoyed.

"I already did. A while ago. You must have forgot." Quinn heads upstairs and curls into bed in his pajama pants. He hates his family. They make him feel stupid and small, like a tagalong; something no one ever wanted and no one ever will. Someone to pick at. Nothing is ever good enough; if it hadn't have been Ellis, it would have been something else. He knows that. It doesn't help.

He tries to close his eyes, but all he sees is bouncing light, the fracture and refracture, blue and cracking gold. That heavy breath. No one cared enough to pay attention to the baby. Henry's dad pulled him out.

He hopes he's asleep when Ellis comes up, but he isn't. His footsteps sound heavy on the stairs, like he's stomping. Quinn fakes it. He stays curled in a little ball, hogging most of the comforter and breathing deeply. Ellis gently tucks the covers around him. He strokes Quinn's hair a little bit, then kisses him on the head, so gently. It's so kind and comforting that Quinn can't help but crave more. He blinks sleepily. "Daddy?" he says in a sleep-addled voice.

"Shhh. Go back to sleep, sweet boy." Ellis tucks him in again. "You're so tired."

"Daddy. Want cuddled."

"Shhh."

"I had a bad day, Daddy."

"I know you did, honey." Ellis takes his clothes off, drops them in the hamper, and fits himself around Quinn. "It's okay. I'm here."

As soon as he feels Ellis naked against him, Quinn gets ideas.

It would feel so good and he wouldn't feel so unwanted. He moves a little and makes a small sound. "Look at you," Ellis says, amused. "Here I thought you were dead asleep and I was safe."

"Daddy, I wanna play," Quinn says, and makes his voice sleepy still.

"You faker, brat," Ellis tells him. "You never went to sleep in the first place.

"I did so!" Quinn protests.

"You did not, baby boy. You've been upstairs waiting for me." His hand moves down between them. "You want Daddy to play with this tight little hole, don't you?"

Quinn moans a little as Ellis strokes his ass.

"You do, little faker. I should spank you for that. I think I will. Get up." He pauses. "And go put on a jock strap. The one that laces up the front, god that's fucking delicious."

"But *Daddy*, I was *asleep*."

"Liar. We both know you weren't. You're going to count six for me. C'mon, sweet boy. Get up. Daddy told you what to do. Go do it." Ellis sounds bossier than usual.

Mumbling, but totally hard, Quinn manages to get on the jock strap Ellis asked for and return to the bedroom. "Look at that big hard cock for me," Ellis says. He palms Quinn hard. "Just how I like it. Grab your ankles, boy."

Quinn knows he's good at this. He never falls, and it never fails to make him so fucking excited. Ellis's hand smacks open-palmed on one of his ass cheeks. "One," he says. Then the other. "Two." It stings, then the warm tingling spreads over his whole ass, and down into his cock. Ellis spanks him lower, then lower still when he counts five and six. Quinn knows his ass is bright pink and he's so hard.

"Quinn, can I take a picture of that cute little ass all pink from getting spanked?" Ellis loves to take pictures, and he always asks. *Quinn* loves Ellis taking pictures. He knows Ellis looks at them later and gets hard.

"Yes, Daddy," he says sweetly.

His cell phone comes off the side table, and Quinn hears the shutter-click sound. “Now get on your knees with your head on the pillow,” Ellis orders. “Spread your legs wide for me, sweet boy.”

Quinn’s still hard in his jock strap. He likes the pressure on his cock. Ellis gets the lube and spreads his legs wide. This is going to feel so good. But instead of lube, Ellis spreads him apart and *licks*. Oh god, that hot tongue on his ass. Ellis laps at him gently, caressing his opening and circling it. Quinn moans. He licks harder, more towards the center; Quinn feels himself beginning to open up, and that’s where Ellis licks, oh *fuck*, his tongue touching just inside Quinn, then *twisting*, then finally fucking in and out of him while Quinn whimpers and begs incoherently. Slick fingers replace Ellis’s tongue. They stroke at Quinn’s ass, circling and petting.

“You love that, baby Q, don’t you?”

“Uh-huh,” Quinn manages. “I love when you do that, Daddy. It feels so fucking good.”

“I bet it’ll feel good when I finger your tight little ass. Do you want me to finger your ass?” Just to make his point, Ellis slips the tip of his finger inside Quinn. Quinn tries to move on it, but Ellis grabs his hips and stops him. “None of that, baby boy.”

“Please, Daddy?” Quinn arches his back, ass in the air. His head’s bent to the side, his eyes squeezed shut with pleasure. He doesn’t want anything but the good feelings of Ellis playing with him. Ellis’s fingers carefully enter him, slide up to the spot he always finds right away, and stroke.

“Good, sweet boy,” Ellis says. “You want another one?”

“Please Daddy? I’ll be such a good boy if you give me another. I’ll come so hard for you. I know you want me to come in this jock strap.”

“That’s a naughty thing to do, isn’t it? So you’d better not come until I unlace it for you and take your cock out.”

Oh *fuck*. “Daddy,” Quinn makes his voice tremble. “I don’t know if I can do that.”

“I know you can do it for me, sweet boy.” Ellis pets Quinn’s cock idly while he slides another finger into him. Quinn tenses a little at the familiar burn of it, but relaxes into it and begs again.

"I don't know if I can, Daddy."

"You will if I tell you to, baby boy," Ellis says very calmly. "You want it now? You want my dick in your tight ass?"

"I want fucked, Daddy, please fuck me. I'll be a good boy and open up just for you."

"Your little hole's all stretched out for me, sweet boy," Ellis says affectionately. "Does it feel good that way?"

"Uh-huh. But I want something in it. Please?"

"Oh, you want me to rub on it?" Quinn feels Ellis's slick cock stroking between his cheeks, against his ass. He whimpers.

"No Daddy, please, please fuck me with your big cock."

"Do you think you can take the whole thing?"

"Uh-huh, I'll be so good and take all of it."

"Now, remember, you don't come until I tell you to, sweet boy."

Ellis is slow and careful, like always, making sure not to hurt Quinn, slipping into him gently, but there's still that familiar painful stretch in the beginning. Then Quinn moans on him as he slides against the good spot. "You want Daddy to fuck you now?" Ellis asks.

"Uh-huh," Quinn says. "Please, Daddy?"

Ellis starts slow but soon he's going faster and faster, holding Quinn's hips while he thrusts. Quinn meets him halfway. He wants it so bad. "Please Daddy," he finally says. "Can I come now?"

"No," Ellis says. "I like fucking your tight little ass right now and I don't wanna finish."

"Please now Daddy?" Ellis keeps stroking against that spot and it's sofuckinggood. Quinn's balls tighten up against his body, he feels like he's standing on the edge of it.

"I said no."

"Daddy, I can't."

"Yes, you can."

"Daddy, I — oh god —" Quinn curls a little, shudders, and comes *hard,* pumping, his cock spasming in that tight space, sticky come all over him. Ellis goes right after, and Quinn feels him thrust, freeze, and spill hot into his ass.

"Quinn," Ellis says, his voice a warning. "That was *very* naughty of you."

"Daddy, I couldn't help it," Quinn pleads.

"You need to control yourself."

"I can't control *that*," Quinn says. "When you're like, fucking me hard and hitting the exact right spot over and over. Jesus."

"You were a very bad boy tonight," Ellis tells him. In a stern, mean voice, too.

Quinn sticks his lip out a little and makes it tremble. He does the baby deer eyes. Ellis has never said anything to him like this before. "But I couldn't help it."

Ellis sighs. "Go take a shower, brat."

Brat. Great. Now he's back to brat status again.

Into the shower. Quinn makes it scalding hot, hot enough to turn his pale skin pink. He stands there for a long time and lets the water run over him. When he comes out, Ellis isn't waiting or reading a book. Ellis has fallen asleep.

Fuck all. Quinn has had some shitty holidays, but this one goes down in history.

He sleeps in the guest room.

Quinn wakes hazy and confused the next morning. It's about ten o'clock. He never sleeps this late anymore; Ellis won't let him. When he pads downstairs in pajama pants, he finds a note on the table. Gone running. Lovely. Quinn snags some coffee, carries it upstairs, gets ready to go out in public, then packs for Tybee. He's laying out a suitcase of clothes when Ellis appears in the doorway.

"Quinn, honey," he says, his voice low, as if he's talking to a frightened horse. "What are you doing? Can we talk first?"

"Nothing to talk about," Quinn says.

"If you're packing, I think there must be plenty to talk about," Ellis says in that same voice. "Let's both take some deep breaths. Why don't you come down and sit and we can talk this out, okay?"

Quinn suddenly realizes what's going on. "Oh sweet Christ, Ellis, I'm packing to go to fucking Tybee. I'm not going anywhere."

"Jesus, Quinn!" Ellis practically yells. "Don't you ever fucking do that to me again, do you hear me? Never! Don't you fucking do that! Do you know how much you scared me?"

"I'm sort of getting the idea," Quinn says dryly. He's not ready to forgive last night until Ellis acknowledges it.

Ellis sort of deflates. "You scared me, baby boy. I thought you were leaving."

"Well, I'm not. I'm going to Tybee for two days with my friends. I've told you like, three times now, Ellis." Ellis is like, willfully forgetting this information.

"And you didn't sleep in bed last night."

"After you called me a brat for no fucking good reason then passed out while I was in the shower."

Ellis sighs. "Quinn. I'm sorry."

"Yeah, well. Would have been nice to hear that last night instead of now. Christ."

"Quinn, I didn't exactly have the best holiday either," Ellis says. He leans against the doorway and watches Quinn pack. He doesn't make a move to come into the room. Weird, for Ellis, not offering to help.

"I'm trying to think of a snarky remark and I can't, so just insert one here," Quinn says.

"You know, my mother isn't very happy I'm basically living with a nineteen-year-old who she hears — well, nevermind."

Quinn's head snaps up. "What the *fuck*?!"

Ellis shrugs. "Savannah talks. So I got treated to very long lectures about my so-called chronic savior complex, my disturbing attraction to troubled younger men, my need to find a boyfriend my own age and settle down, don't I want kids one day, how do I know you won't sell my antiques for drugs —"

"If she *really* knows what she's talking about, she knows I have my own fucking money for drugs, thank you very much. I don't need to take yours." Quinn slams his suitcase shut. "So basically

Mama doesn't want you fucking around with the Rutledge oops baby with the bad reputation?"

"Basically, yeah," Ellis says. "So I got that *all fucking day yesterday*. You think I was in a particularly great mood when I came home?"

Quinn blinks a few times. Ellis clenching his teeth, stomping up the stairs. Calling him a brat and then passing out. He *was* in a terrible mood, and he just took it out on Quinn. "So all that other deeply offensive shit aside, which I'm not even touching right now, why didn't you tell me all this, oh, maybe *last night*? Instead of being a dick to me?"

Ellis sighs. "I should never, ever have treated you that way, Q, and I'm so sorry. But you don't need to deal with my drama."

Quinn roots through his drawer for some decent socks. He's used to stealing Ellis's. "You mean you don't think I can deal with it."

"That too, yeah," Ellis says. When Quinn looks up he realizes Ellis isn't kidding. What. The. Fuck. He's just a little kid to Ellis. That's all he is. A little boy toy. Someone to play with and protect from the world.

Quinn shakes his head. "Wow. This really is, at its core, a fundamentally fucked up and unequal relationship, you're aware of that, right? I mean, if you step back and look at it? You don't think I can even deal with hearing about your *mom*?"

"Quinn, you're so fragile about rejection, that's why you're acting this way right now —"

"You treat me like a fucking broken doll." Quinn slams the socks into his suitcase, as much as you can slam socks, which isn't much and turns out to be deeply unsatisfying.

"And one day we'll have you stuck together again. You're getting there, baby. You're so much better than you were when we met. And it's only been a few months. Imagine where you'll be —"

"I'm imagining, right now, where I'll be in under an hour, which is Henry and Wills's beach house on Tybee."

"Don't leave on a bad note like this, Quinn. I treated you terribly and I'm so sorry, baby. You're right. I should've told you. I should've trusted you with this. I should've remembered about Tybee. Can I take you to lunch and maybe we can talk some more?"

"No, I wanna go hang out with my friends at Tybee, not get bitched at for coming before you deemed it appropriate. Not a fun game, Ellis."

"Then we won't play it again, Quinn. And I told you I was sorry. There isn't anything else I can do, other than try to make it up, try to talk about it some more and work it out some."

"No. I wanna get on the road."

Ellis sighs and runs his fingers through his hair. "Okay. Fine. I'll miss you, Quinn."

Quinn grabs his leather bag. "Yeah. Miss you too, Ellis." Quinn walks past him down the hallway.

"Hey," Ellis says. "Before you leave. Isn't it traditional, no matter how angry one is, when one leaves one's boyfriend for several days, to give him a kiss?"

"I don't know," Quinn snaps. "I've never had one and you know it."

"Then what the fuck am I?" Ellis asks.

Quinn's quiet for a moment. "I don't know. Daddy, I guess."

"I think that falls under the umbrella of 'boyfriend,' Quinn."

"I don't think it does."

"Quinn," Ellis says in his patient and reasonable voice. "You're holding everything at arm's length again because you feel rejected. You felt rejected by your family yesterday and you felt rejected by me and now you're so eager to get to your friends because you don't think you'll feel rejected if you see them. Stop pushing me away. I know you hurt right now. I know you don't want to go to lunch and you don't want a hug and you don't want to kiss me. That's okay. You need to work things out. But before you go, just stop running your mouth. Actually tell me something. Do you still love me?"

Quinn stops. He turns and looks straight at Ellis. "Yes," he says. "You idiot. Of course I still love you. And sometimes, it really fucking sucks." He carries his bag down the narrow stairs and takes his peacoat off the coat rack, along with his favorite cashmere scarf. It's actually Ellis's. He ceded it to Quinn.

"Well, at least you know why you hurt then," Ellis says finally.

"Guess I do." Quinn puts his scarf on, then his coat. He thinks about a hat but it would fuck up his hair. He does toss one in the bag, though.

Ellis stands next to the couch. He looks sad. "See you in a few days, Quinn," he says. "I'll miss you a lot."

"Miss you too," Quinn says. Grudgingly.

"I really wish you wouldn't leave like this. Please let me take you out."

"No."

"Can I give you a hug?" Ellis has knitted his brow; he keeps tucking his hair behind his ear. He isn't looking at Quinn anymore.

"I guess," Quinn says, because he hates to say no when Ellis clearly wants something this much. Ellis crosses the room in about two steps and swoops Quinn in his arms. "I love you, baby boy," he says quietly. "I love you so much. You scared me so bad. Please don't ever scare me like that again. I thought I was losing you."

They've used the L-word, but never this way. Never those little three words. Quinn can't remember the last time he used them with anyone. Probably his mother? But he didn't mean it. He doesn't know if he's ever meant it. It stuns him to hear it from Ellis. Quinn drops his bag and wraps around Ellis, closes his eyes and lets himself feel it. He sits quietly in the moment, in the afterglow of the words, in Ellis's arms, in his good smell and the soft skin of Ellis's neck against his lips.

"You don't have to say it back," Ellis tells him. "It's okay if you don't say it."

"Shut up," Quinn says. "Just shut up." He wraps tighter around Ellis. His scarf (Ellis's own scarf) probably tickles his nose.

So Ellis is quiet. They stand in the middle of the living room, Ellis leaning down, Quinn on his toes. Quinn finally breaks the spell when he rests his head on Ellis's shoulder.

"Why were we being quiet?" Ellis finally asks.

"Because you said it. And I wanted to hold onto that for as long as I could without letting it go, I guess." When he says it, it sounds really stupid. Quinn reddens. "It's dumb. But I love you too. For what it's worth, I guess."

"Quinn," Ellis says sadly. "Stop qualifying everything. It's worth everything to me." He kisses Quinn then, slow and gentle, cupping his face and playing with his lips. Quinn loves being kissed like this. So hard to break it off, but Quinn does it.

"Be good, sweet boy," Ellis says. "I'll be waiting for you when you get back."

"I'll be good," Quinn says. He smirks. "Daddy."

Ellis swats him on the ass as he walks out the door.

CHAPTER 9

Quinn drives his yellow Stingray out to Henry's house on Tybee. Everyone's supposed to be there, a massive blowout with all their friends from high school. Calhoun's shoulder-length brown hair swings in Quinn's face when he hugs him. "Audie isn't here," he sulks. "He said he couldn't think of a good excuse and anyway they always spend Thanksgiving weekend shooting things at his stupid farm."

Quinn's honestly sort of glad Calhoun's hot boyfriend couldn't come; Audie's nice but Calhoun wouldn't notice the four horsemen arriving if Audie was around. Henry's identical twin, Wills is practically sitting on top of Crispin in the hot tub, Crispin's curly head on Wills's shoulder. Henry has some blond guy with him, and they're arguing about something. "QUINN!" Henry yells. "Oh my god, Jax! This is Quinn Rutledge! Quinn, this is my boyfriend, Jax."

"Hey," Quinn says. The guy's about Ellis's height, six feet or so, cut, with spiky blond hair and a ton of freckles.

"You're the video gamer," Jax says. "Bet I can take you."

Quinn snorts. "No way."

"Good thing we brought all the game systems."

"Name it," Quinn says. He can play them all.

"Once I get drunker."

Lucky and Thor Jasper splash around the hot tub, already drunk, impossible to tell apart except by demeanor. Lucky's the one hitting on Isabel, who he dated in ninth grade, and she giggles in a tiny bikini. Delia sits back and rolls her eyes in something a little less risque. Calhoun snuck outside to call Audie, so Quinn changes into his suit, hops into the tub, and wraps an arm around her waist. He kisses her cheek. "Hey, cousin," he says.

"Hey, cousin," she says, and kisses him back.

"You two are soooooo cute," Isa says. "Like bookends. You look like boy-girl twins."

"You say that like, every time we get together, Isa," Delia tells her. "How's Ellis?" she asks Quinn.

"Who's Ellis?" asks Lucky.

"Oh my god, Ellis is soooooo hot and he totally has that Brad Pitt hair thing going on. Quinn, you are so lucky. I hope you pull it." Quinn can tell by her thick drawl that she's already drunk.

Delia smacks her. "Isa! Behave!"

"Wait. Is this the boy toy you were telling us about that time in the bar?" Lucky asks. "The one who wouldn't fuck you?"

Quinn shrugs. "I guess."

Lucky smirks. "Guess he does now. And you know Quinn's not pulling any hair, Isa," Lucky says. "He's the one getting his hair pulled." Lucky reaches over to yank at Quinn's, who smacks him off. God, Lucky can be such a dick. He always liked Thor better.

"You got a guy around, Rutledge?" Wills asks from the corner. "Either of you?"

"Ohmygod totally Quinn does but Delia doesn't," Isa bubbles. "Quinn's is sooooo cute and he's like, how old is Ellis, Quinn?"

"Old enough to drink legally," Quinn says evasively.

"Oh shut *up* he's like totally thirty-five or something." Isa fucks with her strawberry-blond hair, which she'd pulled up in a messy bun so it doesn't get wet.

"Is *that* why you haven't been texting us back to go get trashed?" Lucky asks. "We were wondering about that. You're always all-in to get drunk and then suddenly, like, no Quinn, since like, September. It's been us and Crispin."

"So tell us about your boy," Wills says. "Man. Whatever. I guess man, in this case?"

"He wants a little twink." Lucky snickers.

"Shut up," Quinn snaps.

"Totally does and you know it," he says.

Quinn splashes him.

Calhoun wanders over and slips into the tub with them. It's, like, the size of a swimming pool. "What's up?" he asks.

"Quinn's new boyfriend!" Lucky crows. "Who Isa says is like, thirty-five and has Brad Pitt hair!"

Calhoun turns his big blue eyes on Quinn. "You didn't tell me you were seeing anyone," he says. He sounds vaguely hurt.

Quinn looks down. He still hasn't told Calhoun about Ellis. He didn't really know what to say or how to say it and so just kind of avoided saying anything at all. "Yeah," he says, twisting his hands together under the water. "His name's Ellis. He's an architect with the Melbourne Firm downtown."

"Fancy!" Lucky crows.

"Lucky, will you shut the fuck up?" Quinn asks. "For like, three seconds? Thor, can you make him shut up?"

Thor gives Quinn a look that says, *Have I ever been able to shut Lucky up?*

Quinn puts his head on Delia's shoulder even though it'll make his hair wet. She pets his cheek. He loves his cousin; practically the only bright spot in his childhood.

"What's he like?" Calhoun asks.

Quinn shrugs. "He's nice, I guess." *He said I love you today and I said it back and it was really scary but it was really amazing too.*

"Is he really *that much* older, Quinn? Where did you meet him?"

"Out hunting," Quinn says, avoiding the first question.

"You know guys who're that old and go out with guys our age only want one thing," Calhoun says seriously.

"Yeah, like Quinn's sweet ass."

"Lucky, shut the fuck up," Delia says. "Ellis is really nice."

"It's not like that," Quinn says.

"What, he wants you to call him 'Daddy' or something?" Wills smirks.

"Yeah, right, Wills, I call him Daddy while he fucks me. Totally plausible scenario," Quinn snarks right back, his stomach flipping.

"Well, you don't come out drinking anymore, and you don't go out to the club anymore," Crispin says.

"How d'you know I don't go out to the club?" Quinn demands. He sits up straight again. Delia leans against him this time.

"Just heard it, that's all."

"You know, Gran was asking me what you were up to," Calhoun says. "She was like, really really really interested in what you were up to. This is totally why, isn't it? Because you're seeing some guy who's like, way older than you?"

"I'm sure Savannah has better things to care about than whose dick is in my mouth," Quinn says, intentionally crude so everyone will shut the fuck up. "Anything else y'all wanna know? Calhoun, how was Audie when you talked to him?"

"Oh. He's okay. He hates the farm. So you like, stopped going drinking and hitting the club all the time because of him? Wow, Quinn."

"Quinn has it *bad*," Wills says. "You should've brought him. He could've bought us all booze." Everyone laughs.

"I'm surprised you're even *here* with how much I've seen you out since like, September," Lucky says. "Does Daddy not let you go drinking?"

"Lay off him," Delia says.

"I do whatever the fuck I want," Quinn says.

"Yeah?"

"Yeah, asshole. God, Lucky, you're a lot nicer when you're sober."

"He had tequila," Thor finally says.

"God, Thor! Why the *fuck* did you let him have tequila?" Crispin demands. "Hey!" he yells. "Who the fuck gave Lucky tequila?"

"Oh, one of the other set of identical fuckers? Me?" says Henry's boyfriend, coming around the corner. "He asked for it."

"You dumbass. Lucky turns into a shithead on tequila, Jax,"

Crispin says.

"And how the fuck was I supposed to know that?"

Crispin sighs.

"At least you don't basically live with Jax," Wills tells Crispin. "It's hell."

"Oh, shut the fuck up about my boyfriend." Henry splashes his twin. "I never start on yours."

"Yeah, 'cause there's nothing to start on, and yours is a loud-mouthed punk."

Quinn sighs. Lucky has Thor and Isa has Delia and Henry has Jax; Wills has Crispin. Calhoun has Audie. Then there's Quinn. There's always Quinn, left out again. Motherfucker. Just like usual.

Quinn slips out of the hot tub. "You want anything to drink?" he asks Delia and Isa. They each ask him for vodka shots. So when he makes a scotch and soda for himself, he brings them each one, which they down like frat boys. They ask for another. What the fuck ever, Isa's probably too trashed for it, but Quinn gets out, retrieves the vodka, brings another shotglass for Calhoun, because he's a vodka drinker, and they all start taking Grey Goose shots. God bless Henry's dad for keeping the bar stocked with top-shelf liquor and never bitching when they drink it all. Pretty soon all of them are hammered.

"So tell us more about Ellis," Delia says.

"He's cute," Isa chimes in.

"Yeah, he's super cute," Quinn says. "He spoils the hell out of me. It's super awesome. I love it."

"Quinn has a sugar daddy!" Henry roars. "We always knew you'd find one in the end."

"Shut the fuck up, Culliver." Quinn reddens.

"Ooooh lookit that face! You so do have a sugar daddy! Who won't let you go out drinking! Quinn! You are so fucking dirty!" Henry smacks at him. Quinn ducks.

"I told him, I bet he calls him Daddy," Wills drawls from the corner. He and Crispin are basically on top of each other by now. They never see each other but seriously, just go bang somewhere.

"Speaking of Daddy," Quinn says. "Since y'all won't stop fucking with me, I'm going home to see him." Quinn is tired of this shit.

"Oh Quinn, quit it. You can't drive like this," Delia says.

"Can so."

"Can *not*, and I'll take your keys."

"Can *so*."

"Can *NOT!*" She's out of the tub, sprinting. She gets to Quinn's room first and grabs his keys from the side table. "You're stuck, cousin," she says.

"Motherfucker," Quinn says. He shucks his suit off. Whatever, Delia's seen it before. "I'm going for a walk on the goddamn beach."

"Stay up here with us," Delia says. She sits on the bed while he gets dressed. He drops his suit on the floor and leaves it there. Ellis would throw a fit and spank his ass red.

"No. I'm just going to keep getting harassed by everyone but you and Isa, and Calhoun'll kill me with his concerned face."

"You know they only harass you because they love you."

"Doesn't feel like it."

"They do."

"Yeah, right." Quinn throws on some jeans and a thick sweater, plus that hat he was smart enough to bring. "I'll be in when I'm in. Am I still sleeping with you and Isa?"

"No, you get to sleep with Calhoun."

"I'd rather sleep with you and Isa. Calhoun'll just moon about missing Audie all night."

Delia kisses him and leaves.

She also forgets the keys.

Quinn waits a little while. He quietly packs his bag, carries it down the back steps, loads it in the back of his Stingray and drives back to Ellis's. It's sort of miserable sometimes; the road shifts and sways; the lines don't seem to stay where they're supposed to go. But he makes it. "Ellis!" he yells when he gets inside. "Ellis! I'm home!"

Ellis pads down the stairs in a pair of pajama pants. He stares. "What the *fuck,* Quinn? How the hell did you get here?"

"I drove." Quinn pulls his sweater and hat off. He knows his hair's all fucked up but he can't bring himself to care very much about it.

"Quinn." Ellis looks horrified. "You're plowed."

"Yeah, probably. That was probably a bad decision. Oh well." He flops on the couch. "I was never one for making good decisions. I ought to text Delia and tell her I'm back okay." He pulls his phone out. Ellis snatches it and frantically taps away.

"What the *fuck*?" Quinn demands.

"I'm demanding to know why the hell Delia let you out of there so goddamn drunk."

"Oh. She tried to take my keys and then accidentally left them on the table, so I took them again."

"Well, I told her you were okay. What were you thinking? Are you an idiot? Quinn, there are some things you never, ever, *ever* fucking do! Ever! Driving around drunk is one of them! You might kill yourself, or god forbid, someone else. You wanna have to live with that?" Ellis is yelling at him now. Actually yelling. Quinn has never seen him really yell before. His face contorts into rage; his brows draw down; he reddens. Quinn watches this from far away, because if he sees it up close he'll lose it.

"I got back fine, Ellis. Christ. Calm down. I have a headache and everything was awful and I just wanted to come home to you and now you're yelling at me too."

"Of course I'm yelling at you! You drove from Tybee to Savannah drunk! Why didn't you call me to come get you?"

"Yeah, the last thing I want is for you to show up in front of my fucking friends. That would have been the icing on the goddamn cake, for Daddy to come pick me up." Quinn gives the word an ugly twist. He's surprised, somewhere in the back of his head, that Ellis isn't bitching about his shoes on the couch.

"What are you talking about?" Ellis asks.

"Oh, the massive harassment I got once Isa started talking

about the hot thirty-five year old guy I was dating. Feel good, she shaved three years off you. They wouldn't let it go. 'Bet you call him Daddy,' oh, that was a great one, that hit real fucking close to the bone. 'Quinn has a sugar daddy.' 'You know he just wants that sweet ass'—just what I need to fucking hear, because half the time I think that's the only reason you want me here anyway; that, and because you like it that we share the same fucked up kink. And everyone there had someone but me. I got sick of all of it. So I left."

"I don't give a fuck what happened! You don't drive drunk!"

Ellis said 'fuck.' Huh. Ellis never says 'fuck.'

"Well, I did drive drunk. So that's over."

"You irresponsible brat. I'm taking you home."

Quinn blinks at him slowly. He hasn't been back to his apartment in two weeks. "Excuse me?"

"I said I'm taking you home."

"Oh, I heard you."

"There are some things you don't fucking do. That's one of them."

"Are you breaking up with me?" Quinn's voice rises. "Because if you take me home, you're breaking up with me. After the shit I put up with from my *friends* because of you?"

"No, I'm just taking you home."

"No, if you take me home, we're done."

"Don't make ultimatums, Quinn."

"You just did."

"Quinn," Ellis says, and his voice is not the I-am-being-patient-with-Quinn voice, but an I-am-clenching-my-teeth voice, "when did I make an ultimatum?"

"When you said you were taking me home. And you don't have to take me. I'll just drive there."

"You will not, you self-destructive brat."

"Yes, I fucking will. If you don't want me here, I'm out. I'll be over sometime when you're not, to get my shit." Quinn stands up, luckily steady on his feet, walks to the door, and opens it. He knows somehow that if he steps through it, everything will change. Fuck it.

He slams it behind him. It makes a satisfying sound, something between a slam and a crash, a rattle from the window panes. Quinn digs through his pants, finds his keys, starts up his Stingray, and drives back to his apartment. Not far across town but the red lights are a bitch; he has to stare and stare at them and they double, treble. His parking job might be fucked up, but he makes it back. The apartment echoes miserably. His armoire looks denuded since he took the gaming systems to Ellis's, all sad disconnected wires. Quinn hopes he has enough clothes for the next day. He thinks he does.

He drops his shoes at the foot of the stairs, the way he always did before. Messily. Ellis would hate it, but fuck Ellis. No coffee but the last-ditch instant he keeps for emergencies, plus fake cream. It'll do for the morning. In the bedroom, he yanks off his clothes and throws them on the floor. Quinn walks naked to his shower, which he jacks up as hot as it'll go. He stands under it until his legs shake. He dries off with a towel he finds on a hook, then drops that on the floor, too. His bed isn't as soft as Ellis's. He's cold, so he digs out some old pajamas. And fuck all, he finds his battered old bear. No one's here to see.

He cries for a long time. Everything is bouncing light. Everything is water, heavy, strange breath, water.

* * *

He pushed Quinn too hard.

He should have been honest about his bad mood last night. They never should have had sex. Ellis thought it might help him. He thought it might help Quinn, but he ended up taking his annoyance out on Quinn, and getting mad over a stupid game. What a dick he'd been. All because his mother wouldn't shut the hell up about him hooking up with a teenager. *When are you going to find a man your own age? It's not healthy, Elliston, for you or for him. And you know he was into drugs. I heard from so-and-*

so who heard from so-and-so that ... and you know it would destroy your father. You know how your father would feel about this. And on and on.

Then he had truly thought Quinn was walking out. When he'd seen him with the suitcase, he'd almost lost it.

Of course, then he *did* walk out, and drunk, so score one for Quinn.

He shouldn't have pushed. He should have talked about it when Quinn was sober. They'd never talked about the way his father was killed. Why would they? Quinn had never asked, and Ellis had never mentioned it. Quinn knew his father was dead. Quinn didn't know his father had plowed into a tractor-trailer on I-16 one night on the way home from the bar. But Ellis went off on him. *After* Quinn had dealt with his parents the day before. *After* Quinn had left his friends, feeling lonely and miserable. *Then* Ellis had decided to do what he'd promised Quinn he'd never do: tell him to leave.

Fuck, fuck, fuck.

Ellis can't fix this.

Quinn won't trust him now: Ellis had told Quinn he loved him then kicked him out of the house. He'd broken everything he'd tried to fix. What a fucking mess. He has to go get Quinn.

He'll get Quinn in the morning.

No, he has to go get Quinn now.

Quinn is alone and scared and miserable. Ellis can picture him in the echoing apartment. Quinn might be drinking alone. He might be crying alone. Ellis remembers the hollowness of feeling unwanted, the terrible knowledge of your own meaninglessness. He had always imagined his chest wide open, empty.

Ellis dresses quickly and speeds to Quinn's apartment. Luckily he has a key. He enters cautiously. "Quinn?" he calls tentatively. No one answers. He peers around in the dark; Quinn isn't downstairs. Ellis nearly trips over his shoes at the bottom of the metal staircase. He climbs it and knocks. No one answers, so he pushes open the door. Quinn is curled up in a tiny ball, the way he used to sleep, mounds of blankets piled on him. A small bear peeks out from his arms. His face looks puffy, as if he's been crying, his hair sweaty. Ellis quietly slips his clothes off, down to his boxers, praying to whatever listens to these things that he isn't overstepping, that this is the right decision. He pulls the covers down and settles in with his arms around Quinn. Quinn immediately turns and clings to him. He burrows his face into Ellis's chest; his arms draw up against him.

Ellis feels so sure he's asleep that he kisses Quinn's head and even ventures to stroke his hair. He smoothes it from Quinn's face, all the sweaty strands, the ones stuck there from his tears. They'll just have to try again in the morning. It's all you can do: wake up and start again. Ellis learned that a long time ago. You have to grit your teeth and make a promise and do it one more time every single day. He fucked up. All he can do: try to unfuck it. Quinn feels like a small, hurt thing in his arms.

"You came," a sleepy voice says. "I never thought you would come, ever."

Ellis can't think how to explain it to Quinn. He doesn't know where to start: with his father, or with his anger at his mother, or how he fucked up with Quinn the night before, or how he fucked up tonight, or that no matter what had happened, there was no excuse for him letting Quinn walk out into the night alone.

"I came because I love you," he finally settles on. "And we can talk more tomorrow."

"I love you too," Quinn murmurs, so tired it can't be anything but the truth.

"I'm so sorry, sweet boy," Ellis says quietly into the dark. "I'm so, so sorry."

He doesn't know if Quinn hears him. But he makes a small noise and curls closer. He falls asleep against Ellis like a small child: a limp weight molded against him without fear or defensiveness. Quinn still holds his bear, the poor thing. Ellis tucks his chin above Quinn's head and lets himself, finally, fall asleep.

He wakes before Quinn. It doesn't surprise him. Quinn is probably hungover, dehydrated, and exhausted. Ellis locates paper and pen from a kitchen drawer and leaves a note on the bed: *Gone for real coffee, love E.* He slips out. When he returns, Quinn has curled into a ball again, but a restless one. He keeps reaching for something that isn't there.

"Wake up," Ellis says gently. "C'mon, baby Q. Wake up for Daddy." He smoothes the hair off Quinn's forehead. "I brought you real coffee."

Quinn sits up and shakes his head, like he's trying to remember. "You saw my bear," he suddenly says, clearly mortified, and immediately shoves the battered stuffie under the pillow.

Ellis smiles a little. "Yeah. I saw your bear. What's his name?"

Quinn reddens. "Sparkle and don't you dare laugh."

"Oh, baby, and they say being gay is a choice. I bet you were a fabulous child."

Quinn cracks a smile. "I kept stealing my sister Darcy's nail polish."

"Why don't you wear it now?" Ellis asks over the rim of his coffee.

Quinn shrugs.

"We'll get you some today."

"Really?" Quinn asks.

"Really and truly. Now we need to get you home and feed you and give you headache medicine and wrap you up and take care of you." This is all Ellis wants to do right now: to take Quinn home, to fuss over him and give him whatever he needs, to cuddle him half to death and let him know how much he's loved.

Quinn looks down. "Ellis, I know I shouldn't have — last night — I know it was a terrible decision — but you get sick of it, you know? I couldn't take the ridicule anymore from the only people I thought really cared. It was so much worse because Isa started it."

"Can I tell you why I got so upset and angry, so you understand?" Ellis asks. "I should have told you a long time ago." Quinn looks up. "My father was killed in a drunk driving accident. He plowed into the back of a tractor trailer. You terrified me. On top of my mother yelling at me all day it was just — I snapped and I don't know how to possibly make it up to you."

Quinn's eyes widen. He puts his hand over his mouth, sets down his coffee, and hugs Ellis. "I'm so sorry," he says. "Oh, Ellis. I'm so, so sorry. For your dad and for what I did and for what that brought up and what it did to you."

The Quinn he'd first met would never have done this.

Ellis holds him. "Thank you," he says, and nearly chokes. "Thanks, baby boy."

They hold each other for a long, long time. Ellis can almost feel the forgiveness passing between them, their foreheads touching, eyes closed, wrapped around each other. Quinn kisses his cheek, finally, and picks up his coffee again. "Thanks for this."

Ellis shrugs. "You need it in the morning and that instant stuff is Soviet Russian-caliber." Quinn hasn't moved from the bed yet. His blond hair looks tousled; it sticks out at odd angles, so different from the pin-straight perfection Ellis has become accustomed to. His eyes are huge this morning, grayish-blue, and his T-shirt drowns him. His legs tangle in the light blue jersey sheets, the fluffy blanket. He's wrapped the velvet comforter around his shoulders. And ohgod, when Ellis looks down, Quinn sits with his legs spread and bent at odd angles, which opens the fly of his pajama pants the slightest bit. But that little sliver: just enough for Ellis to glimpse his pink cock.

"Does my boy need anything this morning?" he asks softly. "Or would you rather go without, after everything?"

Quinn looks at him with those big, big eyes. He clearly hadn't anticipated this. "Daddy?" he asks, and he sounds tentative.

"Do you want me to play with you this morning like I always do?" he asks. Ellis craves the normalcy of it, the connection, the small thing he can give.

Apparently so does Quinn, because his wide eyes look begging, but not to get off. It's the look he throws Ellis when he wants cuddling. "Oh Daddy, yes. Yes yes yes."

"Can I fuck my sweet boy? You look too delicious this early. Please let Daddy fuck you. Tell me how you want it, honey."

Quinn looks down and plays with the sheet. "I wanna sit in your lap and ride your cock while you cuddle me, but I haven't been good."

"Did you say sorry?"

He nods and picks at the sheet some more.

"Then take off your clothes, lie down and let me kiss you. Where's your lube?" Quinn points to the side drawer. Ellis is amazed to see several toys in there: plugs, a vibrator, a prostate massager. "Baby boy, you didn't tell me you had toys over here."

Quinn shrugs and reddens.

"Oh, these are coming home with us and you need to show me *exactly* how you use them. And I need to use them on you. But not right now, honey. Right now you're going to lie down and let Daddy kiss on you for a while."

Obediently, Quinn strips and lies on his side. Ellis takes off his boxers. Of course, Quinn's hard; of course, he can't keep his hand off it. Ellis swats it away. "Naughty thing," he scolds. "That's mine to play with." He pulls Quinn close, and the blond hums with pleasure and wantonly rubs his cock on Ellis's before they even start kissing.

"What if I wanted to go slow?" Ellis asks, but the friction's too good, slipping against that improbably big cock on Quinn's small frame. Quinn tilts his chin up, and Ellis kisses him slow and deep, licking and tasting him, sucking Quinn's lips luxuriously. Quinn's arms twine around his neck; one leg goes over Ellis and the other straight down. His nipples have hardened. Ellis leaves his mouth and begins nipping at him; Quinn gasps. He loves this. Ellis bites his neck, his ears, and finally his chest and his nipples, those sweet, hard little nipples he loves. Quinn sucks in a pleased breath and wiggles against him. "You love being bitten, baby boy," Ellis murmurs to him. "Little submissive. Feel how hard that big cock got when I bit you. Stand up and lay over the bed, baby boy."

Quinn's bed is lower than his; Ellis kneels behind him. And oh, he's so indulgent with himself this morning and lets himself bite those delicious little cheeks, holding them in his palms and nipping all over, leaving marks. Quinn whimpers under him, then moans when Ellis spreads him and licks that perfect pink pucker, the one he thinks about when he jerks off — so seldom, now that Quinn keeps him busy. He loves looking at Quinn like this, tiny, closed up, so sweet and innocent, not at all ready to get fucked; Ellis loves knowing he's going to change that. He tongues Quinn in soft circles, drawing patterns on him, tickling the very middle of his hole until he starts to open. Then Ellis licks harder, rougher. He twists at that perfect spot until Quinn whimpers with pleasure, until his tight ridges start to part for him, until he can fuck him with his tongue. He withdraws and slicks his cock, then slips his dick between those small cheeks and rubs the underside against Quinn's entrance. "You like that?" he asks Quinn. "You like it when Daddy rubs his cock on you?"

"Uh-huh, but I want *more*," Quinn whines.

"Like this?" Ellis swirls his soft head at Quinn's hole. "You like Daddy's cock right there?"

"Uh-huh."

Ellis would never, never enter Quinn without fingering him. Quinn knows that. So he makes himself pull back, slick his fingers, and slip them inside, one by one, making Quinn shout with pleasure as he strokes the right spot inside him, then fucks them in and out of his ass, so tight, oh *god* so tight. Ellis stands and gets back on the bed. He sits like Quinn asks. "Come sit on my cock, sweet boy," he says. "You need cuddled and you need fucked, don't you, baby Q?" He slicks Quinn's cock as an afterthought, and Quinn arches up to him.

"I'll be such a good boy for you, Daddy," Quinn says. He scrambles into Ellis's lap and lowers himself, more quickly than Ellis would have entered him. Ellis holds him up and groans with pleasure at his tight ring holding the base of his shaft. Quinn swivels his hips; Ellis knows he's hit the good spot when he cries out and begins fucking him, up and down, held tight and cuddled against him. "You like that, baby boy," Ellis coaxes. "Tell Daddy how good that feels."

"Your cock feels so good in my ass, Daddy," Quinn says. "Oh my god. I love your big cock in me. I love fucking it like this. I wanna come so bad, Daddy. You feel so exactly right in me. I love riding you like this while you hold me. Are you gonna come, Daddy?"

"Daddy's gonna come in your tight ass, baby, if you keep moving like that," Ellis manages. He's getting close now. "But you need to be a good boy and wait. Shhhh. Slow down. You need to learn to be patient."

"Daddy!" Quinn practically wails.

"Quinn. Slow. Down." It's killing him. He wants to come so much. But Quinn does need to learn to hold off and take longer. He fucks like a teenager and that needs to end. The other night taught him that if nothing else. But Ellis also learned he needs to be gentler about it. "Shhh. Now stop. And don't sulk. Wrap your legs around me." Ellis holds Quinn, sets a pillow behind him, and lays him down on the bed without pulling out. Quinn looks surprised. Ellis smirks. "You got what you wanted, little one. Daddy was nice to you. Now it's Daddy's turn. And Daddy wants to fuck his boy on his back."

Quinn pouts, but he starts to make pleased little sounds as his slick cock slides between them. "That's it, sweet boy. Does your cock feel good? You like when I fuck you and it rubs between us."

"Please fuck me harder?" Quinn asks.

"No."

"Why, Daddy? Please?"

"You need to learn to be patient. I told you. Now lie down and enjoy it. Doesn't my dick feel good in your ass? Tell me how good it feels."

"It feels really really good, Daddy. You keep touching just the right spot and my cock feels so good between us."

"Good boy. That's it. Now I want you to try to wait as long as you can. Can you do that for Daddy? Can you be a good boy and wait?"

"I don't know, Daddy. It feels so good."

"You tell Daddy when you're close, okay?" He starts fucking Quinn harder, like he's wanted, that divine ring tugging on his cock. "You want Daddy to fuck you like this? I know you like it when Daddy fucks your tight ass hard."

"Daddy, I'm so close," Quinn moans.

Ellis forces himself to stop. "Shhh. Doesn't Daddy's cock feel good in your ass?"

"Uh-huh." Quinn twists on it.

"No. None of that. Can you feel those big, heavy balls? You feel all the come I'm going to pump into you? I know you want me to shoot all that come into you." He nips Quinn's neck again.

Quinn sighs. "Daddy," he whines.

"You need it now, sweet boy?"

"Uh-huh," Quinn says hopefully. He bucks his hips up, and his cock slips against Ellis's belly. "*Please*, Daddy, please let me come, I'll be so good."

Two times: enough for Quinn right now, especially after all that's happened in the past days. Ellis pins his arms, earning a delighted little sound and a hip shimmy, and starts slow, but quickly begins fucking Quinn harder. "There you go, baby. That's it. You like Daddy's cock in your ass? You like Daddy fucking you hard? Are you going to come all over for me? Let me see how much you come, baby boy. C'mon, come for Daddy. That's it. I feel you getting ready." Quinn meets his thrusts; their balls slap together and his whole body tautens. Suddenly, he cries out under Ellis, shudders, and Ellis feels the familiar hot, sticky spurts shooting from his cock. "That's it, sweet boy. There you go. Come hard for Daddy." That sticky feeling on his stomach drives him crazy; Ellis thrusts deep and loses it, spilling into Quinn, pumping over and over. Quinn arches up like he wants every bit of it, so fucking hot.

Ellis finds washcloths and cleans them off, then tucks Quinn back into bed. "You wanna go back to sleep for a while, sweet boy?" he asks.

"Wanna go back to your bed and sleep," he says. Quinn yawns and cuddles into Ellis. Ellis strokes his hair and kisses him. "Put on some clothes and get your bear."

"I don't need my bear!"

"Do you like to sleep with your bear?"

Quinn reddens.

"Well, then. Get your bear."

He holds Quinn's hand out to the car, opens the door for him, and drives with his hand on his thigh, stroking it. Ellis wants to feed him so much but he seems like he needs sleep. "Are you tired, sweet boy, or do you want breakfast?" Ellis asks him.

"Both?" Quinn says after thinking. "My head hurts."

"How about we stop at home, get you a shower and some clean clothes and some medicine, then see how you feel?"

"Okay," Quinn says.

Ellis pours Quinn water and headache powder and more coffee. He showers with him. He washes Quinn's hair, conditions it, then washes him all over. Of course Quinn gets hard. Ellis ignores him. Quinn gives him those pleading eyes and he still ignores him. And when Ellis dries him off with a big, fluffy towel, he tells Quinn to dry his own cock. "But do it fast and don't play with it," Ellis orders. "That's mine."

Quinn lowers his eyes. "Okay, Daddy."

Ellis brushes out his own hair. He brushes out Quinn's hair and straightens it the way he likes. He picks Quinn's clothes: ripped jeans and a tight T-shirt. He lays out the eyeliner. "Really?" Quinn asks. "It's Saturday morning."

"I'll take you to Loki. You'll blend. You'll also look like a delicious little twink."

They hold hands. It feels important.

CHAPTER 10

Quinn never expected Ellis to show up in his apartment. Much less cuddle him. Much less tell him everything was alright; he was sorry. Then bring him coffee and fuck him.

Ellis really does love him.

He'll take it.

So Quinn doesn't want to let go of him. They hold hands all through Loki. Quinn's playing with Ellis's hand when he realizes something. "This week has sucked," he says. "But it all sucked for one big reason."

"Hmm?" Ellis asks. He's in the middle of crunching the duck confit nachos, and they're hard to talk around.

"No one thinks we should be together. Your mom thinks I'm too young and my parents and friends think you're too old. Everyone thinks we're in it for the sex."

Ellis appears to think about it. "Yeah," he says. "In a nutshell, yes. That's why this weekend has truly sucked."

Quinn looks down at Ellis's hand. "When did you come out?" he asks.

"When I was in college."

"How did you do it?"

"I just ... I started Emory and told everyone I was gay. I told my parents when I came home for Thanksgiving. My mother was livid. My father ..." Ellis is quiet for a moment. "My father told her she could have no son at all or a gay one, and she could fucking pick. He said he loved me no matter what and he fucking knew which one he wanted, and yes he said 'fucking' both times. I cried." He looks away and Quinn knows he's trying not to cry. "What about you?" he finally asks.

"I came out when I was sixteen," Quinn says. "I think everyone knew, anyway. At least, they already called me 'faggot', so one day I just blew up and said, 'So what's it matter that I am?' And everyone heard me. Delia, she already knew. And it was really hard, for a long time. You know how it is, in high school. But I always pretended I didn't give a shit and my friends stuck up for me — Delia and Isa always did, and Wills and Henry, and Calhoun and Crispin. Not like I knew then because the twins are bi and Crispin's gay, but I always kind of knew Calhoun was. But I always faked it and got in people's faces. I told my parents and they pretended they didn't care but you could tell that they did. Mostly they ignored it because, whatever, four other kids, who cares if the youngest is a pansy and a disappointment. The oldest is on the way to becoming a fucking heart surgeon. But even when I knew I'd get beat up, I never stopped throwing it in people's faces. I never shut up, because I wasn't ashamed. Were you ever ashamed?"

Ellis shrugs. "When I was younger. Not later. But it was a different time."

"Ellis," Quinn says. "I don't want to be ashamed of you. I'm not ashamed of you. I mean, I'm not going to walk around telling people what we do in private. But I'm not ashamed to be in love with you." Ellis came to find him. He feels like he can say it now, like it can come out, like he can touch it and feel it without that cold coil of fear.

Ellis's green eyes widen. He touches Quinn's face. "I'm not ashamed of you either, sweet boy."

"So we come out. Like we did before. Like we have nothing to be ashamed of, because we fucking don't."

"See?" Ellis says. He strokes Quinn's cheek. "Judiciously, baby boy. Judiciously."

"The Christmas parties are starting up," Quinn says. He looks at Ellis fiercely. "The first big one is next weekend. It's the Garden Club's thing, at The Narrows. My mother was blathering all about it the other day. You know she's president."

"My mother'll be there," Ellis says. "She's obsessed with her roses."

"So we go." Quinn takes a big drink of his water. Ellis insisted that's all he was drinking, and he's desperately thirsty. "I was ordered to be there anyway. You're my date. I'm dancing with you in front of everyone in Savannah." He pauses. "Most of my friends will be there. Their parents drag them to these things. I know Isa and Delia will be there. Henry and Wills usually are, too. Crispin goes because Wills is there. I'll call Calhoun and *make him* come. His Gran wouldn't miss a party unless she was actually in the ground."

Ellis knots his brows. "Calhoun's grandmother?"

"She knows everything about everyone. If she sees it, everyone will know we love each other and we're not ashamed." Quinn puts his head down on his folded arms. He's suddenly, totally exhausted. "Now I'm tired, Ellis. Can we go home?"

Ellis gets boxes for his nachos and Quinn's hashbrown mess, god bless him. He strokes Quinn's hair and tells the waiter no, he doesn't need to see the bill, just run his card, his boyfriend's tired and wants to go home. Quinn smiles a tiny bit, hearing it. Finally, he stands up, drags himself out to the car — he almost falls asleep in it — and then up to the bedroom. He practically faceplants into bed.

"Clothes off," Ellis says. "I don't care how tired you are. It's barbaric." He undresses Quinn: pulls off his T-shirt, undoes his jeans, and practically peels them off him. "Brat, you didn't wear anything underneath," Ellis says. He undresses and climbs in bed with Quinn, who immediately curls up on him and falls completely asleep.

He wakes a few hours later. They spend the rest of the day in pajamas on the couch. Ellis brought home leftovers from his mom, and seems intent on feeding them to Quinn, who's thrilled to keep consuming stuffing and turkey sandwiches with cranberry sauce while curled under a blanket, with a glass of sweet tea. "I love having you to fuss over," Ellis says. "I don't know what I'd do anymore without you here to baby. I've gotten used to it."

"If you wanna baby me, come back so I can lay my head on your lap again and you can play with my hair," Quinn says. That was so damn comfortable. Quinn loves when Ellis plays with his hair.

"That doesn't mean you get to order me around," Ellis says sternly. "Just because I like to fuss over you doesn't mean I'm a pushover, sweet boy. Or that I'll do whatever you ask. Or that you get whatever you want."

"I know what I *really* want." Quinn smirks. He always wants to.

"Now you're being a brat."

Quinn blinks his lined eyes. "Can I play with my cock, Daddy? It's so hard. Do you wanna feel it?"

"You may *not* play with it."

"Please?"

"I said no. You're obsessed with sex."

"But that's because you're so hot, Daddy. I had my head in your lap and I just wanted to turn around and make out with your cock." Theoretically. He hadn't been *really* thinking about it at the time, but he could have been.

"You're being a tease," Ellis warns from the kitchen.

"It feels so *good* to be this hard, Daddy."

"Upstairs. You knew what was coming."

"Aw, *Ellis*. I was kidding." Great. Now he's going to get *really* hard and Ellis won't do anything about it and he already took a shower so *he* won't be able to do anything about it. Godfuckingdammit.

Quinn drags himself upstairs. He takes his pajamas off, takes off his briefs and his socks, folds everything, and waits. As soon as he hears Ellis on the stairs, he grabs his ankles and waits.

"Oh, look at you," Ellis says. "Are we trying to mend our ways and be a good boy now? Someone feels bad about being a slutty little brat, don't they?"

"Yes, Daddy," Quinn says, as contritely as he can manage, because he *doesn't* feel bad at all and he really wants fucked. Knowing Ellis is staring at his ass right now doesn't help.

"Hmmm. I think another kind of discipline is in order for you right now. Lie down on the bed, please. Put down a towel, because I don't feel like changing the sheets.

Oh. *Oh*. Quinn gets to come after all. He ducks happily into the bathroom, grabs a towel, and lays down. Ellis fits himself behind Quinn, naked except for his boxers, and carefully slicks him. "Tell me when you're close. You're not allowed to come until I give you permission. And don't grind on my cock."

Ellis starts exactly the way Quinn likes. He plays under his head. Then he jerks Quinn slowly, with lots of lube, gliding over his whole cock. He keeps pausing to play with the spot Quinn likes, and when Quinn can't stop himself from moving his hips, and Ellis has to tell him to stop it, goddammit, he begins jerking Quinn *fast*, going over his head, pumping at him.

"I'm so close," Quinn manages.

It stops.

Quinn whines.

"Behave," Ellis says affectionately. "You need to learn to control yourself and this is the only way you will. Shhh." He cups Quinn's balls and strokes them. "Does that feel good, baby?"

"Uh-huh. That feels really good, Daddy."

"Then hush and enjoy it. What about this?" Ellis grasps Quinn's cock. It's not getting jacked off, but it feels really, really good to be held. "Do you like it when Daddy holds your cock for you?"

"Yeah," Quinn says shyly. "It feels good."

"What about this?" Ellis gently strokes up and down the underside of Quinn's shaft. "Tell Daddy how much you like it."

"Daddy, that feels really, really, really good. Will you please touch the spot I like, Daddy?"

"You're being impatient."

"I'm sorry, Daddy." Quinn squirms.

"I told you not to grind on my cock, baby Q."

"I can't help it!"

Ellis *finally* starts rubbing that good spot under Quinn's head again. Quinn sighs contentedly as Ellis jerks him, pauses, jerks him, pauses again, then jerks him *fast*. Quinn bucks up to his hand and feels his body going taut. "Daddy, I'm going to —"

Ellis stops again.

Quinn pants with the effort of holding it in.

"*Please*, Daddy. Please let me come. Please, I'll be so good. Please," Quinn begs. His whole body feels as if he's stretching toward it.

"You can be a good boy by doing what Daddy asks."

"I am! I'm being so good. Aren't I being good?" Quinn wiggles under Ellis's hand, which cups his stiff cock up and against his body.

"Don't you rub against my cock," Ellis warns. Quinn immediately stills. He bites his lip. Once he stops moving, Ellis strokes him, barely, with his thumb. "Shhh. You can wait. Shhh. You can learn to wait, baby boy. He cups Quinn's balls again, holds them. "Do you like it when Daddy holds those?"

"Yeah," Quinn whimpers.

"Just think how much come you have in them for me, sweet boy. When you learn to wait like this, you'll come more, did you know that? Don't you want to come so much for me?"

"Uh-huh, Daddy."

Ellis slips two fingers behind Quinn's balls and pets him there. "You like that, baby?"

"Mmmmm, that feels good, Daddy."

"What a good boy you're being now." Ellis's fingers move back up to that perfect spot and play across it. Quinn makes a pleased sound. Ellis only strokes there for a moment before he begins jerking Quinn hard. Quinn gasps. "I'm so close," he says after a few moments."

Ellis stops again.

"There, baby," he says. "Now let me rub your back for a while so you can calm down. Turn on your belly and *don't* rub your cock on that sheet."

"I don't—"

"Roll on your front, please, sweet boy. You did very well."

Quinn flops over, forcing himself not to huff angrily.

"Shhh. You were so good," Ellis tells him. "You were such a good boy for Daddy. I know, that's so hard for you to learn, Quinn. No one ever taught you to wait for what you want. Daddy's going to teach you to wait." Ellis's thumbs attack the tension in his neck and Quinn groans with pleasure. "That's it, sweet boy. Relax for Daddy. Shhh. Just take deep breaths and calm down." Soon, Quinn's lost himself in Ellis's back rub, in his thumbs and fists and forearms attacking the tension and stress from the past several days. His back cracks over and over. He ends up limp, boneless on the bed, a pillow under his chest so his head can dangle downwards and Ellis can reach his neck properly.

Then Ellis sits between his legs. His hard cock has slipped through his fly, and the soft head touches Quinn's ass. Quinn hums a little to show that yes, he notices, and yes, he likes it. He'd move on it but he feels like jello.

Ellis gets up on all fours, his cock trailing up Quinn's ass and onto his back. There's a tiny bit of stickiness there. Ellis must be *really* turned on; he doesn't drip much. "Baby boy got what he needed," Ellis says into his ear. "Now it's Daddy's turn. Daddy hasn't touched that cute little ass of yours. Can you stand up?"

"Mmmm. If I have to," Quinn murmurs.

"Stand up and grab the edge of the mattress rim, low down, for me. You've been a *very* good boy."

Sleepily, Quinn stands and grips the bottom edge of the mattress rim for Ellis. He knows his ass is in the air, right where Ellis wants it. He feels Ellis stroke it. "You were such a good boy. Shame I didn't turn your cute ass red beforehand, I love it like that."

Quinn feels a lubed finger exploring him and moans. He whimpers and whines on it; all that arousal rushes back. His cock springs up and drips again as Ellis works his fingers inside him, massaging his tight ring. "That's it, sweet boy. Open up for Daddy. I wanna see a nice, open little ass for me." Ellis fucks him with two fingers, then presses them outwards, stretching Quinn. A third slides inside him, that familiar burn with it. Then they're all fucking him, fucking him hard, and Quinn moans on them. They withdraw. Ellis's slicked cock replaces them at his entrance. "Tell Daddy what you want," he says.

"Please let me have your cock, Daddy," Quinn pleads. "You teased me and made me wait and I want it so much. I'm all sticky from dripping for you, Daddy."

Ellis begins to slide into him slowly. Quinn gasps, partly from the usual pain of it, partly from the pleasure of *finally* being filled, of *finally* knowing he'll get to come. "Oh god, Daddy. Daddy, that's so good. I love it when you fuck me, Daddy."

"You were such a good boy, you tell Daddy if you want it fast or slow."

"Daddy do it hard and fast, please do it hard and fast."

"What a good boy you are," Ellis says. He grabs Quinn's hips. "Be a good boy and stay still so Daddy can fuck you." Ellis strokes inside him slowly a few times, but then he's going quick, hitting that good spot inside Quinn and making him moan, fucking Quinn *hard,* all while Quinn begs *more Daddy more, please fuck me more Daddy, harder Daddy I'm going to come for you, can I please please please come for you Daddy?*

"Of course my sweet boy can come for me," Ellis says. "I wanna see my sweet boy shoot all that sticky come. C'mon baby. You want my hot come in your little ass?"

"I love when you come in my ass Daddy, I'm so close, please come in my ass. Please please I love it when you pump hot come in me, Daddy —" Quinn shudders suddenly and lets go, his cock spurting again and again. Ellis buries himself in Quinn and spills. Quinn feels the liquid heat flooding his ass and moans again. Ellis pulls out. Quinn feels the stickiness on his thighs.

"Look at that," Ellis coos. "Look at all the come on my boy's thighs. Isn't that pretty. And you came so much for me. What a sweet boy." Quinn stands and feels more come trickling on his thighs. He wants to play with his cock again. Already.

They clean up and curl up in bed together, probably for the night, Quinn figures. "Daddy?" Quinn says tentatively from somewhere around Ellis's chest. This scares him, bone-deep. But he wants to.

"Hmmm?" Ellis asks, his nose buried in Quinn's hair.

"I love you, Daddy." Quinn's voice shakes a little, but he says it.

"Oh, sweet boy." Ellis tips his mouth up and kisses him. "I love you too. I love you so much. You don't even know. Now get some sleep, baby Q."

Quinn still shakes a little. Ellis strokes his back. Once he starts that, Quinn falls asleep quickly. He feels safe.

* * *

Sunday's more of the same. Sandwiches on the couch. Cuddling. Lazily watching movies. "Do you have a tux?" Quinn asks.

Ellis gives him a look.

"Okay, that was a stupid and insulting question," Quinn admits. "I have to go back to my apartment and get mine."

"Yeah, this running between apartments thing — it's getting old," Ellis says. "I've been meaning to ask you, since you're here every night anyway, if you wanted to just move in. You know, all your stuff. Store what doesn't fit."

Quinn draws back from him on the couch, where they were tangled up watching some stupid movie, and stares. He can't think of anything to say so he doesn't say anything at all. He hasn't lived with anyone but his parents. He knew he didn't want to deal with the SASA dorms, and he didn't want to ask any of his friends and get turned down.

"You can say no," Ellis says hastily.

"Can I bring my velvet sectional?" he manages: a stupid question but it's all he has.

Ellis sort of smiles. "I think we can find a place for it, yeah."

"Then yeah?" Quinn says tentatively. "If you really mean it?

Do you?" He's so scared Ellis just tossed this off, that he'll reconsider; that he wasn't actually serious about it.

"Okay, baby Q," Ellis says. "How about you give up your lease on the first of the year and we move you in through December?"

Quinn burrows back into him and if he pulls the blanket mostly over his head and his eyes leak a little, Ellis pretends not to notice. But he does, and strokes Quinn's back for a long time.

Delia calls him later that night, just before bed. "I feel really bad about this weekend," she says. "I hate that you felt like you had to leave because we teased you about Ellis."

"You didn't do the teasing," Quinn says. "Anyway, we're going to the party at The Narrows together next weekend. Just so everyone can see us. And we're going to fucking dance, too."

"Oh my god. You aren't."

"We fucking are," he tells his cousin.

"You ballsy son of a bitch," Delia says admiringly. "I love you, Quinn Rutledge." She pauses. "What's your hot boyfriend think of this?"

"My hot boyfriend's all in."

"Good for him. Imma tell everyone, you know that, right?"

"You better."

"I love you, Quinnie."

"Love you too, Deal."

Ellis looks at him, amused. "I'm your hot boyfriend, huh?"

"*I* think you're hot." Quinn uses his sweet voice. "I think you're really hot, Daddy."

"I think I liked looking at you yesterday in that eyeliner and those tight jeans," Ellis says. "I think I liked it a lot. Put them back on for me, little twink."

Quinn's stomach butterflies. He goes upstairs and does what he's told.

"Oh, now that's hot," Ellis coos at him. "Look. At. You." Then Ellis has him up against the wall. "You're short," he says, and picks him up. Quinn wraps his long legs around Ellis and twines his arms around his neck. "That's it, sweet boy," Ellis says in his ear. "You hold onto Daddy." His mouth crushes down on

Quinn's, and Quinn grinds against him, hard from the sucking and nipping, the tongue in his mouth and the hard press of lips against his own. "I want those jeans off and *only* those jeans off," Ellis orders. "Knees on the couch and your hands on the top edge of it. I wanna see that cute ass in the air. And I'm not feeling patient, boy. Stay like that for me while I get the lube."

Quinn pulls off his jeans, scrambles up on the couch, cock at full mast, waiting. Ellis comes back downstairs. "That's it, sweet boy. That's what Daddy wanted. You want Daddy to play with you now?"

"Please, Daddy?" Quinn asks. The position excites him, his ass so exposed to Ellis.

Quinn hears Ellis opening his jeans and pushing them down, and oh god he's going to fuck him with his clothes on, so goddamn hot. He must slick himself, because suddenly a wet cock slips between his cheeks. Ellis rubs himself there. "You like that?" he asks."You cock feels so good, Daddy. Rub it on my ass, please Daddy?"

"What, like this?" Ellis nudges it at his entrance and begins opening him with it. Not all the way, but enough, enough that Quinn feels himself stretching and even burning a little with it, but so good he leans into it. "Little slut," Ellis says. "You want it so bad." He smacks Quinn's entrance with his cock. "Naughty boy. Be good for Daddy or I'll turn your cute ass red."

Then the lovely stretching, finger after finger, touching that good spot and fucking him while Quinn begs: *more Daddy more fuck me harder I love when you finger me, finger my ass harder I'll be so tight for you, want your big fat cock, I promise I can take it all.* Then Ellis slides into him for real, Quinn's tight muscles stretching with the familiar burn of taking him. Almost pleasure now, and Quinn arches back to him.

"I want you hard and fast, baby boy," Ellis says.

"I'm dripping so much for you Daddy. Do you want to feel? I know you like to feel it when I drip."

Ellis leans forward. His fingers graze Quinn's cock. "Slutty boy. You always want it. Daddy's going to give it to you. You want

Daddy to do it?"

"Uh-huh. Do it hard."

Ellis starts slow. Ellis always starts slow, and he's hitting the good spot, Quinn quivering with pleasure at it. But then he grabs Quinn's hips and fucks him fast and hard, holding him still, nails digging into Quinn's soft skin. "Good boy," he manages. "Good boy to take all of Daddy's cock. Daddy's gonna come in your tight ass until it runs down your thighs. You want that? Tell me."

"Come in my ass, Daddy, please?" Quinn says sweetly. "I like to feel when you come. It's hot inside me and it feels so good."

Ellis shudders and suddenly there is it, the warm pumping spill in him, spurts of it as Ellis thrusts again and again. He slows and pulls out, then lets Quinn up. Ellis pulls up his jeans and does up his belt.

"Pick up your clothes and go upstairs, baby," Ellis says. "You need me to clean you off after that." He's right; Quinn feels his thighs sticky. He hopes he's going to get off sometime fucking soon, but he won't ask. If he asks, it won't happen.

Ellis turns on the shower, strips, and steps in. He motions for Quinn to get in too, but hogs all the goddamn water. Then he switches with Quinn, kneels down, and cleans off his thighs. "And look at this cock," he scolds. "Big and hard and sticky. You dripped so much for Daddy." Ellis gently cleans Quinn's cock while he sighs with pleasure and drips a little more. "Now stop that," Ellis scolds. He washes the rest of Quinn, hands wandering all over him, touching and grabbing and stroking. Ellis gets out first, then holds out a towel for Quinn. This time, Ellis carefully caresses Quinn's cock and balls; he slowly circles Quinn's ass under the guise of drying him. Quinn bites his lip with pleasure. "You like that, don't you? Aren't you just Daddy's slutty boy? Do you need something?"

"Mmm-hmm, Daddy," Quinn says, with his wide, innocent eyes. "My cock got so hard when you fucked me."

"It did, didn't it?" he says conversationally.

"Will you play with it for me, please Daddy?" he asks.

"What a good boy you are," Ellis says, kissing his forehead. "You didn't complain when you didn't get anything right after, you let me play with your cock in the shower and you didn't beg, and you didn't ask until I asked if you wanted something. What a good boy, Q. Go lie on the bed for me, honey. You've had a long few days."

Quinn stretches out on the bed. Ellis curls around Quinn and holds him tight with an arm slipped under his neck and around his chest. "Do you need Daddy to play with your cock, sweet boy?"

"Uh-huh, please Daddy?" Quinn says. He's already hard at the idea.

Ellis cups his balls, then strokes them. "Are you gonna come a lot for Daddy?"

"I'll come so much for you, Daddy, I promise."

"You know I like to see a lot of sticky white come from my boy." Ellis runs his hand up and down the underside of Quinn's shaft. He still hasn't bothered with lube. "I love a fat cock on a twink. Twinks with big cocks also seem to have more trouble keeping their hands off them."

"I've been so good about that, Daddy. My cock's yours and I'm not allowed to touch it."

Ellis kisses the back of his neck. "Aren't you a good boy." His hand closes on Quinn. "I bet you need something first, don't you?"

"Daddy, can you put lube on me?"

"Of course, sweet boy." Ellis slicks him then, and Quinn arches up to his hand.

He goes so fast. Ellis tries to tease him but Quinn wants it so much it doesn't work. As soon as Ellis starts jacking him fast, Quinn curls up, makes a small sound, and comes all over Ellis's hand. Ellis coaxes him to come more just the way he likes: *That's it, baby boy. Come harder, Daddy loves to see his boy come. Get it all out for Daddy.* Quinn finishes, spent, and Ellis cleans him up. He turns Quinn around and cuddles him, then pauses and grabs Quinn's bear for him. Quinn snatches it.

"You never saw my bear," he says.

"What, a bear named Sparkle?" Ellis asks. He kisses Quinn on the head. "Go to sleep, baby."

CHAPTER 11

They spend the rest of the week in a comforting normalcy, a beautiful, beautiful routine that Ellis wants to catch hold of and never let go. They wake up early, and now it's always sex. Quinn seems to crave the connection, and Ellis can't resist giving it to him, even if they can't curl back up together afterward. Then protein bars and off hunting, the sun rising over the fields, breath steaming in the cold but the horses warm beneath them.

They change quickly at home, Quinn simply ditching his shirt and jacket for a fleece vest and sweater, helmet, gloves, and riding crop in hand. Still delicious. "I love you," he tells Ellis, kisses him, and runs out to his car. Ellis loves that moment: that unselfconscious, tossed-off 'I love you'. So easy, so everyday. This is what he wants. This life. He hasn't told Quinn but it's something he's never had either. Not like this, not this simplicity with another person. He's had boyfriends, of course. But never this; never the running kiss, never the 'I love you' as he sprints out the door with the coffee mug Ellis hands him.

Ellis dresses in his suit each morning and thinks about what this means for him, for Quinn.

Four glorious days of this, in between getting their tuxes cleaned and their shoes shined, in between the intoxicating knowledge that on Saturday night, they're telling Savannah she can go straight to hell. Four days of sex in the evenings, of cuddling on the couch, of dinners out and in. Four perfect, perfect days.

On Friday they hunt in the morning, a perfect, crisp day for dressing up in wool, wearing leather gloves, and trotting atop a warm horse, while the frozen dew crackles underfoot. After the traditional port toast before the hunt begins — Ellis hands his to Quinn, as usual — they pass a flask of brandy back and forth. Ellis sips; Quinn drinks. Quinn looks delicious dressed up in his tattersall vest, stock tie and gold pin, dark navy jacket, buff breeches and high black boots with garters. Ellis wears the same, but with a canary vest. They both have on tan gloves and safety helmets.

"I miss wearing pink," Ellis comments as a member of the staff rides by in a scarlet jacket.

"Only staff here," Quinn says, as if he's scandalized. "Alexander Culliver wears it — Henry and Wills's brother. He's only, what, twenty-two? But he does all that stuff with the hounds, when he's home, and walks the hounds out, and clears trails and does all the rest of it. I'm too busy to bother." He grins. "But I'm just happy to go out on horseback early in the morning and take jumps and ride. I love listening to the horns and the fussy etiquette and everything." He blushes, and Ellis realizes he's listening to the real Quinn; to something he's never told anyone. "It's one of the best things, to be on a good horse first thing, especially on mornings like this, when you can smell the cold and the horse is warm and there are good jumps."

Ellis smiles. "It is, isn't it?"

Quinn pats Mister. "And he's one of the best ones, you know? I trained him myself, mostly, too. I didn't buy him this way. I used to hunt Lucifer. I think he misses it. I should bring Isa and Delia out more often."

Ellis holds Quinn's hand until they pick up the pace again.

"Are you excited for tomorrow?" he asks Quinn as they canter up to a jump.

Quinn laughs. "I can't wait. I can't wait to see their faces. Calhoun's Gran is going to die." He laughs again, looking at Ellis instead of the jump, so he's off, he's not paying attention, and when Mister leaves the ground he's not ready, he's laughing, looking at Ellis, but suddenly he's not. Quinn's tumbling, falling, headfirst and then an almost dream-like flip onto his back, falling down, down, his head hitting—

They don't move him. You're not supposed to move someone when they're unconscious and there's a possibility of spinal injury. Ellis can't touch Quinn; he doesn't dare touch Quinn, and it's breaking him slowly to see him, so still, but so beautiful in his hunting gear, not a mark on him. He wants to pick him up and walk away. He can't.

They have to use a helicopter, can't get the ambulance out into the field. It adds a terrifying sense of urgency: when Ellis hears it coming, the whipping sound in the air, the chopping noise, he knows in a visceral way that something has gone horribly, terribly wrong. No, Ellis can't ride with them. He has to walk to the end of the field where the Master of Foxhounds picks him up and drives him to his car, and he has to use Quinn's cell phone to try over and over to get in touch with his parents. Everything has a nightmarish, dream-like quality to it, as if he's fallen down a rabbit hole, falling and falling, as if he's hit some terrible wonderland where nothing will ever be the same again. He finally manages to reach Quinn's father at work.

Ellis can hardly get the words out. He manages the bare details. Fell. Bad. Very bad. Helicopter, unconscious, Savannah Memorial, now, right now.

He has to drive himself. He makes it somehow, breaks all the speed limits on these winding country roads, and floors it through downtown. Ellis has never driven like this. He swore he would never drive like this. But Quinn's face: so goddamn still, so pale.

Quinn could breathe. At least he could breathe.

He makes it before Quinn's parents.

Ellis is frantic. They have Quinn in the ER. He's alive. He's breathing. Something about his brain, the way his head hit, one in a million chance, wearing a helmet like he was, so rare but it happened, he hit in just the right way, back of the head. His brain is swelling. They have had to open his skull to relieve the pressure and is Ellis family and can he consent to medical procedures? The words spill over him, almost meaningless. Quinn, Quinn, Quinn. He wants Quinn.

Quinn's father appears. He consents to whatever is necessary, sits and waits. He does not go back to see Quinn. Ellis begs to see Quinn. They refuse. He eventually sits, head in his hands.

He should call work.

"I suppose you're Ellis, then?" Quinn's father asks, finally.

"Yes," Ellis says without lifting his head. "You'd be Alexander Rutledge, then."

"Yes," he says.

They're silent for a while.

"My wife *is* on her way," he says eventually.

"Uh-huh," Ellis says.

More silence.

"Don't you think you're a bit — old — for Quinn?"

Ellis looks up at this man. He has Quinn's hair, but short, Quinn's blue eyes, but smaller, the same pointed chin, but a much larger frame. "I'm in love with your son," Ellis says. "And right now I'm absolutely fucking terrified for him, so if you could shut the fuck up about anything along those lines until he's okay again, I'd be deeply, deeply grateful." He drops his head again.

Quinn's father doesn't answer. Ellis didn't expect him to.

Eventually Quinn's mother sweeps in. "Stella Rutledge," she says. "You must be Ellis Ashford."

"Ma'am," he says, and stands, because Ellis may be physiologically incapable of *not* standing when he meets a woman.

"Well, how is he?" she asks her husband.

"The same."

She heaves an exasperated sigh. "Do I have to do everything, Alexander? Jesus Christ." She marches over to the nurse's station. "I'm Quinn Rutledge's mother. I want to speak to his doctors. Now."

Quiet conversation, then a raised voice. "Oh, I'm certain it's *quite* possible. It *needs* to be possible. You will *make it* possible."

They take her back. She emerges twenty minutes later.

"He's the same," she reports.

"Did you see him?" Ellis asks. He can't keep the desperation from his voice.

"Yes. He looks horrid. I only looked for a second. He doesn't know we're there anyway."

"What does 'the same' mean?"

"Fluid on the brain now. Shunt. Coma. No change. They'll call when there is one."

"Are you — are you fucking *leaving*?" Ellis asks.

"I am. His father'll stay. We'll all alternate so someone's here all day. Darcy'll have to come back from Brown if this goes on. Poor thing."

Ellis decides that, as Quinn once said, they don't exist in his world. He approaches the nurse's station. "I'm Quinn Rutledge's boyfriend," he says. "I was with him when he fell. Is there any *possible way* I can see him, even just peek in at him? Please could you go back and ask? I'd be so grateful."

She nods and disappears. A minute later she returns. "Come on then," she says.

They hit a button on the other side of the double hospital door with an audible metallic smack. Everything here feels contaminated, germ-filled. The doors swing open. Another nurse meets Ellis. "You can stay as long as you want," she says. "What's your name, honey?"

"Ellis," he says, and his voice almost cracks.

"Ellis, you stay with him as long as you need to. And talk to him. We don't know what he can hear. We're going to move him soon, into a regular room. You can come with him then. I'll let the nurses up there know the situation."

"I'm so grateful, ma'am."

She stops and looks Ellis in the eye. "I was in his brother Alexander's class at St. Albert's. My parents were at the party when he nearly drowned, and my mother always said it was a goddamn shame the way they treated him." She turns and keeps walking. "Quinn's right in here, Ellis." She touches his shoulder before he goes in. "You know, some of us don't give a flying fuck how old you are."

"How do you —"

"People talk." She shrugs. "Even to me, and I'm a nurse and hence a goddamn disappointment. I'm going to warn you. He doesn't look great. That doesn't mean he's at death's door. But he doesn't look good, Ellis. Okay? They had to shave his head, too, fair warning."

She pulls the curtain and lets him in. Oh god, Quinn's so pale, curled on his side, wires and tubes and terrible things Ellis can't look at. Quinn would faint if he saw them, and all his pretty hair cut off. It'll grow, Ellis tells himself. It'll grow.

She said to talk to him.

Ellis sits in the white plastic chair, oddly like a lawn chair, the kind you see sold cheap outside a discount store. Incongruous in this setting full of beeping machines and tubes and monitors, high-tech — things — keeping Quinn alive. "Hi baby Q," Ellis says quietly. "I'm here. It's okay. I'm here, love. They finally let me back and I'm here."

He doesn't know what else to say, other than to cry. He doesn't want Quinn to hear him cry.

"I never told you what happened after my father died," he says. "I didn't want to. You were right, the other day. I sometimes treat you like a broken doll and it's not fair. You're not. You're so strong, baby boy. I saw your parents and I see now, how strong you must be, if you lived through that. I can't imagine how lonely you must have been. You never told me you nearly drowned, baby. You never said. You have to tell me that story when you wake up. The nurse just said it. She said her parents were at that party when it happened.

"My dad died when I was nineteen. The very beginning of my sophomore year of college, like the first day of class. I still managed to get my shit done. But ... baby boy, I wasn't exactly real stable to start with, back then. I didn't have a lot of friends at college, and the ones I had were partiers. So when dad died, I kind of ... got lost. You've never asked me how many guys I've slept with, I know, because you don't want me to ask you the same question, but the truth is I don't know the answer, baby Q, because the number's so high I lost count. I always, always stayed safe. I never, ever drank, because of my dad. But god, did I do whatever drugs I could get my hands on and I fucked my way through half of Atlanta. I almost failed out of Emory. I had to do an extra year and they pulled some serious strings to get me into Duke. My dad was an alumnus and I know that's what did it in the end.

"I always felt so miserable and empty, Q. I'd forget for a while and then it would come back and I'd go to bed alone, every night. And then the boys. The gorgeous, gorgeous boys I'd want to love. I'd want them to need me, and they'd walk out and break me every time."

He talks and talks. He tells Quinn about Logan. He tells him about Mark. He tells him about Bhavin, about Tyrone, about all the beautiful boys who walked away.

They move Quinn into another room. Ellis goes with him.

"But then you came along," he says. "And you didn't leave. And you wanted to be there, and you needed to be loved, and I could love you, I could help you, and once you got better we would love each other more and more every single day." Everything is quiet. "I just want to be a good daddy," he whispers. "I just want to be the best daddy to my sweet boy."

Quinn never moves. Quinn never looks at him, or opens his eyes, or talks. His eyelids flutter. He excitedly calls the nurses.

"Oh baby," she says to him. "That's an automatic nerve reaction. He can't control that. It's not indicative of any higher brain function, sweetie."

That's when Ellis realizes they don't know if Quinn will ever wake up. He excuses himself and walks down the corridor. His boots echo horribly; he's still in his hunting get-up, but unraveling, stock tie undone, jacket off, shirt untucked. He walks into a private waiting room, sits on the couch, and sobs brokenly.

He gets up eventually. Quinn needs him.

Four hours after Quinn is moved into the other room, his mother arrives. She stands awkwardly in the doorway. "You're here, then?" she asks.

"Yes," Ellis says.

"You're not leaving?"

"No."

"I can't look at him like this. I'll be in the waiting room. Will you come get me if—"

"Yes."

She leaves.

A few hours later, a slim, dark-haired man in a nice suit appears. He walks in and sits next to Ellis. "Mother went home. I'm Thomas. You must be Ellis. You know, you have no right to —"

"I know." Ellis simply cuts him off.

They sit in silence for several hours. Thomas reads a book and messes with his phone. Ellis holds Quinn's hand and scrolls through his phone with the other, reading *Sherlock Holmes* short stories out loud.

Twenty-four hours later, Ellis has glimpsed Quinn's brothers Alexander and Tristan, both of whom elect to pop their heads in, but stay in the waiting room. The nurses make him go home with orders to eat and change and sleep. They swear they will call him if anything changes, they know they aren't supposed to but they promise.

Ellis's phone starts to ring after two hours of sleep.

He doesn't know how they get his number, but they all start to call.

The numbers pop up: Henry Culliver first.

"Is Quinn okay? Is he okay? Do we need to come down? Is he alright? Our mama just told us."

"How did you get —" Ellis asks in a sleep-addled voice.

"Is he *okay*?"

"No," Ellis says in a miserable monotone. "He's not. He fell while out hunting. Hit just the right way. They had to bring in a helicopter."

"Will he —" Henry's voice gets quiet. "Will he wake up?"

"They don't know."

"We're coming over. Can we come over?"

"I don't know if they'll let you see him," Ellis says wearily.

"Oh, they'll *let us* see him."

When Ellis arrives, he doesn't see any of Quinn's family. About five minutes later, two enormous dark-haired guys walk in, bizarrely doubled. Their hair looks artfully fucked up; they dress like frat boys and carry flowers. One stands in the doorway and looks horrified. The other bursts into tears. "Oh, Quinnie," he says. He kneels down next to the bed. "And we were so awful to you. I'm so sorry, Quinnie.

"You must be Ellis," the one in the doorway says eventually, his voice shaking. "I'm Wills Culliver. That's my brother Henry. He's — he's one of Quinn's best friends, I guess. He always says Quinn is one of his, I mean."

A guy with long brown hair, past his shoulders, opens the door. He immediately closes his eyes. "Ohmygod," he says. "Ohmygod. Gran told me it was bad but she didn't say it was this bad. Oh god Quinn. Oh god. I came as soon as I could get here from Charleston. Oh god."

Something about this guy seems so fragile, so in need of protection. Ellis can't help himself. He stands and hugs him. "Hi," he says gently. "I'm Ellis. You must be Calhoun. You can talk to him. They said they don't know what he can hear and it might help, if you talk to him."

"Hey, Calhoun," Wills says quietly.

"Hey Wills," Calhoun says from Ellis's hug. He's not letting go, this one. He starts sniffling. Henry's still crying, kneeling on the floor, holding Quinn's small hand in his large one and talking quietly, words Ellis can't hear. Then Calhoun's crying, too.

"Delia —" he starts. "Delia's coming. She said she's on her way. They didn't call her and she's so so so mad, Ellis. Isa's coming with her. She's desperate to see Quinn." He swipes at his eyes and steps back. "I'll be right back. I need to make a phone call."

Henry stands up. "You can go home, brother. Imma stay here

for a while."

"You sure?" Wills asks.

"Yeah. That okay with you?" he asks Ellis.

Ellis nods.

Calhoun comes back. He also kneels and talks to Quinn for a long time. "His brother Tristan is here," he says. "He's in the waiting room reading. I said you were back here and he said you were welcome to sit and wait as long as you wanted but that he wasn't going to sit and just stare at Quinn." He shakes his head. "Gran says they're awful to Quinn."

The door fairly bursts open.

"Quinnie," Delia says. She bursts into tears, but immediately approaches the bed, takes his hand, and starts talking to him. Isabel slips in behind and bursts into silent, awful tears. Ellis just takes her in his arms. She turns into him and cries.

Delia ignores everyone else in the room. She talks to him for at least half an hour, stroking her cousin's hand, before she stands up. "Tell me everything and don't lie to me about his chances," she says to Ellis.

Isabel detangles herself, sniffs, squares her shoulders, takes Quinn's hand, and begins talking to him quietly. She pets his forehead.

Ellis tells Delia, and tells her the truth.

"C'mere," he says. "Your mascara's somewhere around your nose about now."

She swipes at it. "I don't give a flying fuck." She turns back to her cousin. "You are going to wake the fuck up, Quinn Rutledge," she informs him fiercely. "You are going to wake the *fuck* up. Do you hear me? I don't care if it takes you weeks but you are going to do it and you are going to be fine, so help me god. You will absolutely *break* me and you will break Ellis and it looks like you'll break Calhoun and Henry too. So get the *fuck up,* cousin."

Delia marches out. Isa stands. "Bye, y'all," she says, her voice shaking and barely audible. "Thanks for staying with him. I guess I better go be with Deal." She follows her best friend out.

"Jesus Christ," Ellis can't help saying.

"Delia punched Tucky Kitsen in the face when he called Quinn a faggot once," Calhoun says quietly. "She got suspended, and half the school brought her class notes for the work she missed."

"She was always telling people off for Quinn," Henry says in a deep rumble. "And yelling at him to wake up — that's just Delia." He sort of laughs. "You should see her boss Isa. And her yelling at Lucky the other night to shut the hell up, when he was —" Ellis thinks Henry realizes what he's about to say and looks down, embarrassed. "When he was making fun of him. About dating someone older. Isa brought it up but she didn't mean anything. She was just saying how cute you were." He sort of laughs again. "God, she can be so spacey."

Calhoun kind of smiles. "But she's a kind of spacey you've been in love with since tenth grade."

"Shut up, Calhoun."

This is what Quinn needs. If he can hear them, this is what he needs to hear. He tells them so. It almost makes him cry. "You know, he thinks a lot of the time that y'all ... that you don't care."

They both look horrified.

"Oh my god," Calhoun says. "Does he really think that?"

Ellis nods.

Calhoun starts to cry again.

Henry looks down. "I should've called him and messaged and stuff more. I forget, y'know? You get busy. And Quinn was never one to sit on Facebook all day."

"I've been calling Audie and going to see Audie instead of coming to see Quinn," Calhoun says. "And when he calls I only talk about Audie. I bet he thinks I like Audie more than him. It's not true. I like them different is all. God. How could he ever think that?" Calhoun swipes his face. "When we were at the twins' birthday party this one time, when we were little, it was time for cake and ice cream —"

Henry actually laughs. "And the two of you refused to come out of the bounce house."

"And my Gran and his mom had to come in and get us out and

my Gran whaled on my butt in front of god and everyone. You know she smacked Wills with her purse after his valedictorian speech."

"Why?" Ellis asks.

"He said 'damn' in it."

"Let's be straight," Henry says. "She smacked him like, multiple times. This was a beating. I remember Quinn laughing his ass off."

"He was so proud when he got into SASA," Calhoun says. "That was all he wanted. Horses. They wanted to ship him off to some Ivy League school or something but he dug his heels in and said no he wanted the horses and that was all. And so he worked out the deal with his parents."

"What deal?" Ellis asks.

Henry looks at him strangely. "Quinn never told you?"

Ellis shakes his head.

"He gets all the land from the farm. Like five hundred acres, everything but the house, plus the money to pay the taxes on it. No one else wants it. And he's going to breed horses there eventually. I can't remember what kind. He always says it'll take him time to turn a profit but goddamn if he hasn't run the numbers. He showed me once. The math works out."

Ellis almost spits his bad hospital coffee. "He never talked about it."

Calhoun looks at Quinn. "I'm not surprised," he says quietly. "Quinn doesn't like people to know how much money he has and how much he's getting. It embarrasses him. I think because the staff mostly raised him so he grew up with people who didn't have it, you know? So he's quiet about it."

Ellis realizes Calhoun is right. Quinn might wear expensive things and buy them, but he never discusses it or flaunts it, and it's always very quietly tasteful, in a way people wouldn't necessarily notice if they didn't know what they were looking at. Like his suits: bespoke but only obvious if you know suits very well. He's never seen Quinn go on a shopping binge, and if he picks up the bill at dinner, he does it without a word. His phone isn't the latest model; he drives that Stingray he loves like a child — he always says he saw it in a dream — rather than something expensive and fancy. It's not even that *fast*. "I dreamed it was yellow and I was driving it down East Bay," he told Ellis once. "You have no idea how long it took me to find it."

"He told me once he dreamed his car," Ellis says inanely.

"Oh my god, he scoured, like, Georgia and Alabama and South Carolina and half of Florida for that thing. Finally found it in some tiny-ass town in Carolina, up near Aiken. I remember driving him up to get it. That shit was in Deliverance country, swear to god. I was waiting for the banjo music," Henry says. "We were seventeen, senior year. His parents had offered him like, something high-end or whatever but you know Quinn. He dreamed that motherfucker and he wanted *that car* and only that car."

They all stare, suddenly, at the boy — the guy, Ellis reminds himself, the man — curled so pale and quiet on the bed, all the tubes. So quiet.

"I don't know what I'll do if he never wakes up," Calhoun says suddenly. "I would never forgive myself for Friday night. He was so happy about you and we just made fun of him because you were older. But his parents, they're outside and you're in here and I can see it on your face. You're the one who really loves Quinnie."

Ellis hurts for Quinn, for the way his family treats him. He doesn't answer. They don't exist in his world.

"They're so horrible to him," Henry says softly. "They always were."

"They don't exist in my world," Ellis blurts, the way Quinn did that day, the one that feels so long ago now, morning mist still dropped down on the field in front of the kennels. Him atop Mister, perfect form. God, that boy can ride.

Henry smiles a little. "That's pure Quinn. Have you heard his other one from Lady Chablis?"

Ellis knots his eyebrows.

"Two tears in a bucket, motherfuck it," Henry says, almost gleefully.

Ellis smiles a little for the first time. "I've never heard that one."

"He used to use it all the time in high school when it would get bad. He'd brush everything off with it. Doug Moray hit him, they wouldn't change in the changing room with him — he'd square up his shoulders, give you that look — you know the one — and just say, 'Two tears in a bucket, motherfuck it.'"

Ellis doesn't know what look.

"Maybe you can tell me something?" he asks Henry. "The nurse mentioned it to me? Quinn never told me he nearly drowned as a kid?"

Calhoun and Henry stare.

"Oh my god," Henry says. "My dad was the one who fucking saved his life. He was like, two, and fell in the pool at a party. Everyone thought everyone else was watching Quinn. My dad said he looked down and there was just this tiny thing all alone at the very bottom of the pool. And it took him a second, you know? Then he realized, and he dropped his drink and dove. He pulled Quinn up and Quinn opened his eyes, tried to breath and choked. He said it was horrible, you could see Quinn trying so hard to breath but he couldn't, but they kept him hanging on, I guess he could breathe just enough or something, until they got him to the hospital. He was there for a long time.

"Daddy says it scared him more than anything in his life," Henry says, "except me not breathing when I was born. It's why we don't have a pool."

Ellis looks at his baby Q and wonders what else he doesn't know.

Eventually, he has to go home and sleep. He won't be able to drive home if he doesn't. They don't call. No change. He brings back Quinn's bear. Calhoun sits in a chair when he returns. "You're good, to be here with him," Ellis says.

Calhoun looks at him with those ocean-blue eyes. "I love him too," he says. "His brothers and parents just sit in the waiting room. One of them's always here. But they don't sit with Quinn. They poke their heads in and see if I'm still here and then leave."

Days. Ellis takes family medical leave.

On Christmas, he sits at Quinn's bedside as usual. His family troops in as one, parents and brothers and sister. Ellis has never seen Darcy before. "Poor Quinn," his brother Thomas says.

"Oh god." Darcy closes her eyes and turns her back. "Mother, you said it wasn't *that bad.*"

"It's Christmas and your brother is in a goddamn coma and you will *show some respect!*" she snaps. She takes Quinn's hand for a moment and strokes it. Ellis watches her face. Something like regret flickers across it, something like guilt. Then it's gone.

They leave. They do not acknowledge Ellis.

CHAPTER 12

Quinn dreams.

The light bounces and fractures. His breaths are always heavy and strange, but everything's so clear and beautiful. Except the people. The people look like far away blurs, but he knows them: Ellis. Ellis is always there, almost always, peering down into the pool. Henry. Calhoun. Sometimes others: Delia and Wills and Isa. Weirdly, he can hear them from down, down in the depths. He can't move, the water weighs down his arms and legs, almost comforting. But he can hear them talk. Ellis tells him so many things, especially when the others disappear. *I love you, I love you, I love you, you will wake up and I love you, your horses are getting fat with no one to ride them, baby boy. Delia and Isa take out Lucifer and Zelda sometimes. Wake up please wake up. You're such a good boy. Come back so I can be a good daddy again. It's all I ever wanted. Please come back Quinn.*

Henry and Calhoun tell stories and sometimes they cry. All of them plunge their hands into the water, but Quinn cannot reach them. He tries. But it's so far away. Wills asks him to wake up, please wake up Quinn. Isa talks softly about the horses and how much they miss him.

Delia yells at him. She comes and she yells and she cries and she stamps her feet.

Ellis tells him about partying. About his father dying. About boys who came and went. About loving him, always about loving him, about the simplicity of handing him coffee in the morning, which for some strange reason, makes him cry.

He can't let Ellis cry.

Ellis can't cry.

Quinn tries hard, so hard, so *goddamn* hard, and he blinks. He blinks on purpose, deliberately, and he squeezes Ellis's hand. He is trying to say: don't cry, Ellis, I love you, Ellis, I am trying, I am trying so hard to be good but this is so so hard down here in the depths, where the water presses down and breath is a strange thing.

Ellis breaks down.

No no no no.

Quinn tries harder. He has to. He *has to.* Suddenly he opens his eyes. Bright and white, white white. White walls, white sheets. White curtains. "Baby boy," Ellis breathes. He frantically starts pushing buttons. "Don't look," he says. "Look at my face. Look at me. Don't look at *anything* else. You fell riding. You've been out for a month. Look at me."

Nurses bustle in.

Quinn glances at his left arm. It prickles. There's an IV in his skin. His vision tunnels back to black.

He wakes to Ellis yelling. "I told you! I *told you* to cover any IV he could see without bandages! Every single time, because he has a terrible needle phobia!"

"His parents consented, Ellis."

"Who do you think knows him better, me or the family who never comes back here?"

"We'll wrap him up now."

"Baby Q, close your eyes so you don't see," Ellis tells him. "But you're going to have to get used to it, okay? Bit by bit. You'll be here a while."

Ellis tells him what has happened. His hair is gone and Quinn cries.

"It'll grow, pretty boy," Ellis tells him. "You'll look adorable in spikes and it'll grow." He whispers. "Little twink."

Quinn smiles a tiny bit.

Everyone shows up a day later. *Everyone.* And they cry. They actually cry. Quinn's stunned. "You weren't a dream," he says. "I heard you calling me from the bottom of the pool but I couldn't reach you." He looks at Delia. "You kept yelling at me, Deal."

She bursts into tears again. "Well, it fucking worked, now, didn't it?"

Quinn has to stay another two weeks but they finally let him go. Ellis takes him home. He's had Quinn's things moved while he was out. "You can rearrange however you like. But I needed to do it." He chokes. "It meant you would come home."

"I heard your voice almost the whole time," he says. "You never left, did you?"

"I had to go home to shower and sleep, but no, as little as possible. Calhoun stayed. Henry stayed a lot, too." He pauses. "And Henry's mom knows it. And Calhoun's Gran knows it. And you know what they say about Calhoun's Gran. I hear it's all over Savannah that I kept vigil by your bedside for a goddamn month." He smiles a little. "Much better than one dance, wouldn't you say? Little drama queen."

Another month of physical therapy and generally being cuddled on the couch. His friends come over a lot, and call, once they go back to school. Ellis doesn't play with him. "You need your rest," he says. Quinn worries it's because of his hair; because he's so thin and pale. It's starting to grow back now, but it's not the long, gorgeous blond it once was. Ellis assures him that he loves it and spikes it up for him in the mornings. He puts eyeliner on Quinn. "You look delicious," he assures him. "I'm exercising admirable self-restraint." He also buys Quinn nail polish.

"I promised you a long time ago," he says. "I got you black and blue and purple. I hope that's okay. Tell me if you want another color."

"No, those are perfect," says Quinn.

"Now, what do you want to do with yourself this semester?" Ellis asks. "You can't do class. You've missed too much. I was thinking ..." He trails off and looks down. "I was thinking you could get a colt, once you are strong enough. If you wanted. And break him. Or two of them, if you think you could handle it. Maybe two ex-racehorses. And you missed your exams, so ..." He trails off again. "I'm sorry Quinn. But you'll have to repeat a year."

Quinn sighs. He's already thought of this. "It's okay," he says. He's already pulled Zelda and Lucifer from the SASA stables and had them moved to his regular boarding facility, the farm next to Henry's house. Not Henry's mom's best friend's, but the one on the other side. It has much better training facilities.

Ellis begins going to work in the mornings. But it's different. He doesn't want to take Quinn hunting yet, doesn't want him on horseback quite yet. "Soon, baby boy," he keeps saying. "Soon." All his friends are gone or working, except Crispin and the Jasper twins. Ellis still doesn't play with him. "You're still recovering," he says. "*Your brain swelled up,* baby Q. I get worried for you, doing anything too strenuous. It scares me."

"The doctors say I'm fine!"

"I'm scared for you, baby Q."

Every night, Quinn gets stiff on him. Every night, Ellis ignores him. "Daddy?" Quinn begs. "Please Daddy?"

"No," Ellis says firmly.

"*Please*, Daddy. I'm so hard for you."

"Baby boy, no."

Quinn just jerks it himself in the shower. He suspects Ellis does too.

But Ellis still doesn't have to be at work until eleven, so they sleep late-ish. Ellis makes them a real breakfast, then goes for a run. Quinn is not permitted to join him.

"You never told me you almost drowned," Ellis says casually one day.

It feels like a gut punch, but he deflects it. "You never told me you fucked half of Atlanta," Quinn comments. "Don't think I don't remember most of that stuff you said to me while I was out." "But you never told me. Henry told me the story, while you were out."

While you were out: like Quinn fucking went to dinner or something.

"Yeah. I almost drowned. Henry's dad saved me." Quinn hugs himself.

"That must have been really awful. Do you remember it?" Ellis asks.

Quinn's quiet for a moment. Then he figures, what the fuck. If he can't tell Ellis, who can he tell? "I see it. When I get upset. I see the bottom of the pool. The whole time I was out, I was in the pool again. When I went home, that night? I kept closing my eyes and seeing the light in the bottom of the pool." He fucks up his spiky hair. "I know that's really weird. I'm sorry."

Ellis is staring at him.

"What?" Quinn asks, panic starting to drop down. Ellis thinks he's crazy.

"You never used to say anything. You never trusted me enough to say anything. And you just gave me something — a glimpse into something no one gives anyone else, or almost never. Thank you, baby. Thank you for that."

Calhoun texts Quinn all the time now. But he calls one day in February. He's cackling. "My Gran—" he can barely get the words out he's laughing so hard. "My Gran — oh my god, Quinn, it's so hilarious. She was asking about your boyfriend. And how he was. And talking about how *amazing* he was and how *spectacular* and what a *saint* and everyone knows he never left your bedside and oh my god, Quinn." Calhoun's laughing and laughing. "No one cares if he's sixty-five. Everyone's like, apparently, totally in love with him being in love with you. At least Gran is. She wants him to come to *dinner* next time I'm home."

They're invited, of course, to Gran's Mardi Gras party. She throws it every year, and every year, all of Savannah shows up. "Guess we get to break out the tuxes after all," Ellis says with a wry grin.

"Yeah, guess we do," Quinn says. "You actually gonna let me go?"

"Wouldn't miss it, baby boy."

The party's scheduled for the beginning of March. Ellis has their tuxes cleaned again, their shoes shined — only the women wear masks, though the men dress rather loudly. Quinn picks out a lavender bow tie and cummerbund; Ellis wears dark green. Gran's house on Forsyth Park glows with lights, all purple and green and gold. A valet takes their keys out front. They walk up the long front steps and are shown into the ballroom, where they walk past two footmen. Only Gran would hire footmen. Ellis and Quinn hold hands.

Quinn knows he looks thin; they had to take in his tux. His hair stands in spikes.

A strange hush falls over the room. Suddenly — Quinn never knows who, he suspects Henry's dad — starts clapping. The whole ballroom picks it up, a thunderous applause that rings from the high ceiling and echoes off the wooden floors and the walls, unmuffled by the green, purple, and gold buntings. Quinn blushes and looks down. Ellis draws him closer. Gran and Calhoun finally approach them; the applause peters out and dies.

"You came!" Calhoun says. "We weren't sure if you would make it!"

"I told you, I'm fine," Quinn says.

"I like your hair." Calhoun grins and reaches out to touch it. Quinn ducks and smacks his hand. Calhoun smacks him back.

Gran hugs Ellis, then holds him at arm's length. "Well," she says. "You certainly proved your worth, didn't you?"

"Ma'am?" Ellis asks, and Quinn realizes they've never met.

"Gran, this is my boyfriend, Ellis Ashford. Ellis, this is —"

"Oh, I know who he is. I remember him as a little boy, though he probably doesn't remember me." She smiles. "Your father would've been proud of you, the way you stayed with Quinn. You know how important things like that were to him."

Ellis looks down and Quinn sees his eyes shining. "Thank you, ma'am," he says, his voice quiet: he's trying not to cry.

"And *you*." She smacks Quinn's leg with her cane. "How are you feeling, sir?"

"I'm fine, ma'am. Just skinny, because he won't let me do very much."

She snorts. "Overprotective, is he?"

"Oh god yes," Quinn says.

"Well, you deserve it after — everything." She waves her hand in the air. "You know what I'm talking about. Look, there's your mother, bless her heart. I'd best shut my mouth or I'll be putting my foot in it." She sweeps off. Calhoun stays.

"Lovely to see you out and about, Quinn," his mother says. She wears a floofy cocktail dress and a half-mask. "Ellis."

"Ma'am," Ellis says.

"You were quite right you know, at Thanksgiving," she says in a business-like way. "He is a nice man and he does treat you well."

"I'm glad you realize that, Mother," Quinn says dryly. "Took you long enough, didn't it."

Isabel appears, looking gorgeous in a champagne dress with a cut-out back. She kisses Quinn on the cheek. "I love you," she says. "But I'm dancing with your boyfriend now, because he loves you too. And he's hot." Ellis suppresses a grin as one of the prettiest girls in the room leads him out to the dance floor.

"You and me, cousin," Delia says. "Is that weird?"

"No, because I love you," Quinn says. "Remember when we did cotillion and I stepped on your feet and you stomped on mine on purpose?"

"Try not to do that," she says dryly.

Quinn whirls Delia around the dance floor, then Isabel. He finds himself next to Ellis again. "Do I get to dance with you?" he asks shyly.

"Oh god, don't make me lead," Ellis says. "Can we wait for one of the slow dances so we basically just stand there and do a box step? I can manage that."

Quinn laughs and laughs.

Then Henry's mom steals Ellis. He hangs out with Calhoun and fends off questions from everyone. Yes, he's fine. Yes, he's healed. Totally okay. He and Calhoun finally sit at one of the tiny tables and end up sort of holding court. People keep bringing him champagne and toasting to his health. Henry's dad won't stop bear-hugging him. "I kept thinking I fished you out of that goddamn pool and you had to make it, Quinnie," he says.

His wife swats him. "Daniel, leave the poor boy *alone.* He's been through enough trauma without you reminding him of that godawful pool."

Even his brothers are forced, by Savannah in general, into a forced politeness. They talk to him more than they've spoken to him in years. Quinn wishes they would shut up and go away.

His mother dances with Ellis. It would look weird if she didn't.

"How was *that*?" Quinn whispers afterwards.

"It was weird dancing with someone who didn't exist in my world," Ellis replies. He kisses Quinn's forehead.

Quinn laughs and laughs.

Eventually, he dances with Ellis. Everyone's so drunk by then that mostly no one notices, and Delia cuts in on them to steal his boyfriend. He shoots her daggers.

"I love him too," she snaps.

"Hello, boyfriend!" Quinn says.

"I'm allowed to love him because he loves you so much, so move. Calhoun looks like he's about to sneak out and call Audie again. Go make him have fun or something."

They take an Uber home. They've had too much champagne to drive. It takes them half an hour to work their way out of the room with all the congratulations and the well-wishes.

At home, Quinn's wearing pajama pants, legs folded beneath him, reading, when Ellis comes into the bedroom. Ellis stares.

"What?" Quinn asks.

"Oh, baby boy," he breathes. "I can see just the littlest bit of your cock through your fly and it's absolutely delicious. And you're better now. After that party, I know you're better."

Quinn ignores him.

"Oh, baby Q." Ellis is practically salivating.

"How's it feel?" Quinn asks as he turns a page, even as he hardens.

"What?" Ellis asks.

"Getting told no."

"Quinn," Ellis says sternly. "Daddy wants to play with you."

Quinn can't help it. He hardens further.

"Mmm-hmm. Your cock's betraying you, sweet boy."

Quinn ignores him. The words swim on the page.

"Take your clothes off and lie on your stomach. Now," Ellis says in that deep, commanding voice. "Daddy wants to play with his boy and he wants to do it now."

That voice. It never fails to make Quinn obey — and make him totally stiff. He pulls off his clothes and lies on his stomach, totally self-conscious; he knows he's lost muscle since he fell, that he's skinny rather than cut, and his hair's short and spiked instead of that gorgeous fall to his shoulders. Ellis strokes his back. "Daddy needs to feed you more, baby Q," he says.

Quinn reddens. "I'm sorry I'm so skinny, Daddy."

"Now that you can ride, it'll come back. And your hair will grow. But I like the spikes too." His voice gets soft. "But you're my beautiful boy. And Daddy wants you. Daddy wants you *bad*. Are you going to be a good boy and let Daddy finger your tight ass? I want my boy with his head on the pillow, up on his knees with his cute little ass in the air."

Quinn feels Ellis touch him, circle gently. He must have already slicked his finger. "You like that, baby?"

"Daddy *please*," Quinn begs, and it's been so fucking long, so goddamn long, and it's all he wants. "Daddy do it fast and do it hard. Make me all nice and slick for you and then fuck me until I come hard, *please* Daddy."

Ellis uses so much lube, and he's careful, but it burns more than before as he stretches Quinn. His fingers make Quinn feel more full than they used to, and they have to wait while he breathes through it and Ellis tells him what a good boy he is: that's it, so good and so sweet to take it like this. C'mon baby. Then he's fucking Quinn with three fingers, so gently at first, then harder and faster, and when Quinn starts to moan with it, he stops.

"Do you want it, baby boy? Tell Daddy."

"Please Daddy?" Quinn asks breathlessly. "I'll be so good."

"But you've been a bad boy. I know you've been playing with your cock in the shower, and it's mine." His cock smacks on Quinn's entrance. "I think you need to count three for that, one for each month, please, and thank me so much for being generous to you."

"Thank you, Daddy," Quinn says immediately.

Quinn feels a hard smack on his bare ass, then the warm, spreading feeling, stinging, straight to his dick. He whimpers a little with it. "One," he says. The other comes, ohgod. "Two," he counts. He can't last like this. "Three," he manages. "Daddy please please please fuck me, I'm so sorry and I'll be so good now."

"Look at that little pink ass," Ellis says. He rubs his now-even-harder cock on Quinn. "You want this, baby Q?"

"Please, Daddy," Quinn begs.

Ellis enters him so slowly. His muscles stretch, oh god they stretch, like he's never been fucked, and he has to breathe through it, make himself relax. "I'm so sorry, baby," Ellis says. "It'll feel good in a minute. I know it's so much right now."

Quinn feels too full, oh god, way too full, stretched out, but slowly, as Ellis strokes his back and talks to him, it starts to recede. He touches that good spot and the pleasure takes over. "You need it carefully, baby boy," Ellis says. He rocks inside Quinn. Quinn whimpers and keens and begs. Ellis shushes him. "You think I don't want it like that too?" he scolds. "Patient. It'll happen."

It builds and builds as Quinn twists on Ellis's cock, as he begs, pleads, meets his thrusts halfway, until Ellis finally picks up a slow, regular rhythm. It's amazing and Quinn arches on him with pleasure. Ellis goes a little faster, and a little faster, until he's fucking Quinn and Quinn's getting *loud*; their balls slap together. Quinn's whole body stretches to reach it, and finally explodes. It's like something electric, these shudders that go on and on, the stickiness shooting from him and then Ellis coming inside him, digging his nails into Quinn's hips and thrusting.

He pulls out. "Lie right down for me, baby," he says. "You were so tight. Lie down. I wanna do something about that right now for you, okay? So it doesn't hurt next time?"

Quinn obediently lays on his belly. "Here, baby boy, this'll help," Ellis says. Quinn feels a very lubed something, a little smaller than Ellis, slip into his ass. "If you sleep with that in once in a while you'll get used to it faster."

It feels amazing. It moves when Quinn moves and he gets hard again. But Ellis cuddles him to sleep anyway.

Quinn has a wonderful dream. In it, he lies on his belly, and Ellis fucks his fingers in and out of Quinn's ass. It feels *so goddamn good* he can't help but rub his cock against the sheets, which earns him a stinging smack on the ass, one on each cheek. He startles awake. Ellis kneels between his legs. Quinn's ass is lubed; Ellis is already fucking him with three fingers. "Look who woke up," Ellis comments. "Someone was rubbing his little ass against Daddy in his sleep and wanted it so much I couldn't help it."

Something *so hot* about waking up in the middle of it. Quinn realizes he must have been so open because Ellis took the plug out while he slept. "Pull that pillow under your chest, sweet boy," Ellis orders.

"I'll be so so good," Quinn promises. He yawns.

"You tell me what you want right now." Ellis's fingers slip out of him.

"Can I have your cock, Daddy? I'm so sleepy and it would feel so good to get fucked."

"Right here?" Ellis's cock nudges at his entrance. "You want it right here, sweet boy?"

"Uh-huh," Quinn arches up to him. His dick rubs deliciously against the sheet. He's getting sticky with precum. Then he realizes his ass isn't just sticky with lube; it's sticky with Ellis's come from earlier *ohmygod.*

"Can you take all of Daddy's cock?"

"I wanna take the whole thing, Daddy. I want your whole big

thick cock."

Ellis pushes inside him, more quickly than usual, the pleasurable pain sharper than normal, until he reaches that good spot and lays on top of Quinn. Then he starts those little tiny thrusts, the ones that hit right against Quinn's prostate, over and over and over, the thrusts that make Quinn buck and moan and shout. "That's it," Ellis says. "I want to hear how good my boy feels. You tell Daddy how much you like it."

"Love it so much when you fuck me, Daddy. Love when you fuck me. Love you. Love getting fucked. I love you, Daddy. Fuck me harder. Please fuck me harder I love you so much I want your hot come in my ass, please Daddy please come in my tight ass, please Daddy I love you Daddy, fuck me harder —" Ellis strokes against him one more time, hard, and Quinn loses it, spraying all over the mattress, all over his belly. Ellis tells him to keep going, keep coming, I want all that hot come from my boy, that's it, until he freezes and shudders himself, pumping into Quinn. Quinn raises his ass up to take it all.

"What a good boy," Ellis breathes. "What a good boy you are." When he pulls out, he cleans them both up and scoots Quinn off the wet spot. Quinn still feels drowsy, heavy.

"That was the first time," Ellis says quietly, drawing Quinn close to him. His arms feel so good wrapped around Quinn.

"What?" Quinn asks sleepily. He has Ellis, and Ellis gave him his bear, and they're tangled together in a pile, warm and comfy under the down. *Are you a sleeper? I don't know. I think so?*

"The first time anyone ever said they loved me in the middle of sex," Ellis says.

"Well, that's the first time I've ever said it in the middle of sex, so we're even," Quinn yawns into his chest.

"That's when you know someone means it," Ellis tells him. "When they say it then."

"You know I mean it, Ellis." Quinn nuzzles into his neck. He smells good. Quinn laughs a little. "Everyone in Savannah knows we mean it now, too — according to your mom. And Calhoun's Gran, so you know it's true."

"You know, sometimes I look at you, and I think, god, I waited my whole life for this. I know that sounds stupid to you."

Quinn opens his eyes and touches Ellis's face. "No," he says. "It doesn't. I feel like that every single day." And when he says it, he knows the truth of it, knows that he waited forever for Ellis to come and take his hand. And not just to be special to *someone*, but to be special to this particular man, this kind and gentle man. "We fit, Ellis."

"We do, sweet boy." Ellis cuddles him closer. "No matter what it looks like to anyone else. We fit."

"And now everyone knows it," Quinn murmurs. He begins to drift off again. Ellis feels so warm, hard and soft in all the right places.

"I love you, Q baby," Ellis says, so softly.

"Love you Daddy," Quinn murmurs. "Love you so much."

ABOUT THE AUTHOR

Julia Mcbryant

Southern born, Southern bred, and when she dies, she'll be Southern dead, Julia loves gold glitter, brand-new pens her children haven't stolen, and notebooks full of character details.

She would like to be finding whelks on the beach at Tybee, admiring the hand-sized moonsnails at Botany Bay, eating oxtail in Rome, or drinking liquor while her husband barbecues a pig. This sounds a hell of a lot more redneck than it actually is.

She also enjoys unicorns, caffeine, and unicorns on caffeine. Julia can generally be bribed with bacon, very good guacamole, and anything related to David Bowie, who is remains alive in all of her books.

When she isn't writing she's writing.

Facebook: https://www.facebook.com/juliamcbryant
Facebook page: https://www.facebook.com/authorJuliaMcBryant/
Facebook group: https://www.facebook.com/groups/2752839774743605/
Twitter: https://twitter.com/juliamcbryant
Instagram: https://www.instagram.com/authorjuliamcbryant/
Pinterest: https://www.pinterest.com/juliamcbryant/

Linked In: https://www.linkedin.com/in/julia-mcbryant-b682661a0/
Goodreads: https://www.goodreads.com/author/show/19186436.Julia_McBryant
Bookbub: https://www.bookbub.com/authors/julia-mcbryan
Amazon: https://www.amazon.com/Julia-McBryant/e/B07S838TFX/

SOUTHERN SCANDAL SERIES

I Wish I Were Special

While my wham, bam, thank you ma'am party-boy life has me failing out of college, I don't tell anyone I really have a daddy kink — that I want (need) someone (much) older to make me flush the coke in my pocket, break me of my smart mouth, cuddle me to death, and keep me so, ahem, busy I forget about the club. Deep down, I'm desperately lonely. I wish I were someone's special boy.

Maybe someone like Ellis: twice my age and sarcastic as h*ll. He wants more than one night. He's persistent. And when he cops to a "savior complex" I practically melt. He wants to help me. I just might take him up on it...

The first of a six-book series, this gay age gap novel does not end in a cliffhanger and has a guaranteed HEA.

Beautiful Boys: Quinn, Ellis, And Amory

Quinn:

After seeing Amory perform in Mama Mia!, we run into him at a BDSM club. Party for three, anyone, with me as the brat? Amory's always wanted a daddy and a boy. But he's from red-dirt Carolina and freaking out over our money. Ellis is down with two boys; we're in love, but there's jealousy... and wrangling... and adding this smart-mouth switch? Way more than I bargained for. So is his scary secret ...

The second of a six-book series, this gay age gap novel does not end in a cliffhanger and has a guaranteed HEA.

Christmas Cousins: Quinn, Ellis, And Amory

Quinn, Ellis, and Amory are all settled in for the Hallmark family Christmas before the boys leave for the Culliver twins' three-day Christmas party on Tybee — Quinn's cousin Baylor in tow, and Delia soon to meet them. Ellis only tells his boys one thing: BEHAVE WHILE YOU'RE GONE.

The beach house looks like pipe bomb of tinsel and fake snow exploded. The hot tub has multi-colored blinker bulbs strung up and set to disco. As the liquor passes from hand-to-hand, Delia and Baylor turn from Quinn's staunchest allies to terrible teases who embarrass him at every turn. As Quinn's misery reaches a Scrooge-ish rock-bottom, something has to give. Christmas is about family. But what happens when your family sucks?
Southern Scandal's novella Christmas Cousins tells the story of the same party detailed in Southern Seduction's What Christmas Means and Low Country Lovers's Learning to Love Christmas. All three novellas should be read in the context of their series, but differ enough in details and perspective to be read together.

Remember All The Things You Don't Want To Forget

This collection of short, impressionistic vignettes tells the story of how they got there. Told in McBryant's lyrical, almost dream-like prose, Remember All the Things You Don't Want to Forget shows how small events in Quinn, Ellis, and Amory's lives — and sometimes not-so-small-events — shaped them, and brought them, almost inevitably, to one another.

These short snippets show their lives before they came together, and offer a glimpse of how the three fit together. Rather than short stories, these are small moments in the lives of three people who came to love one another — three people who were waiting for each other all along.

Dirty Little Secrets: Quinn, Ellis, And Amory

Ellis:
I've got two boys — enough gay kink for anyone. But Quinn sucked his thumb until fifteen, sleeps with a bear, and mentions a certain superhero T-shirt and undie set he had as a kid ... so I mention some hot age play.
Baby boy appears in bed with a book and a bear.
And it's been a long time since I've been topped. But Amory switches ...
Amory says he'll definitely switch for Daddy. And he's gonna make Daddy beg.

The Weight Of Familiar Objects: Quinn, Ellis, And Amory

Ellis is a good daddy. He always swore he'd never pick.
Then he thinks he has to.
It's a simple thing. Just a piece of paper, really.
And all hell breaks loose.
Ellis makes a decision that leaves Quinn with all the money — and Quinn can't cope. A college graduate who's been handed the farm of his dreams, he can't adult, and he thinks it's tied into his age play and their daddy/little dynamic. Amory's off on a Broadway tour. Ellis is trying to pick up the pieces. Quinn's desperate for Ellis and shoving him away. The threesome is fraying at the seams, and all of them seem powerless to stop it.
The last Southern Scandal novel, this does not end on a cliffhanger and guarantees the daddy you expect, the boys you love,

and the HEA they all deserve.

Made in the USA
Columbia, SC
04 May 2024

35292299R00112